"Emily, did he hurt you?"

She noted the concern.

"Call the police," the man hollered as he stood inches from Emily, his dark eyes filled with an alarm that touched her.

"And an ambulance," her rescuer continued. For a man just three years out of his twenties, Cormac Colton had way more confidence and authority than she'd have expected.

Cormac. He was really there, not just a figment of her way-too-harried state of mind. "I don't need an ambulance," she said then, finding her own stash of commanding tone as the light changed again and she stepped off the curb to cross the street.

"Emily." He reached for her shoulder, not with force, but in an attempt to keep her there. "You need to talk to the police."

"I'm fine, you can go." She gave him as much of a dismissive tone as she could muster despite shaking harder.

Someone had just tried to kidnap her!

And the man who'd dumped her had suddenly shown up out of thin air to save her?

Dear Reader,

Welcome to New York in February! While I've never lived in New York, I have friends and work associates who do, and I love it here. I also love the Coltons. The family, the bravery...they grip me every time. And this time, I'm visiting something else with which I have personal ties—the world of prosecution. My only child was a federal prosecutor and I held her hand through most of her law school days. Public lawyers are a special breed. The hours they have to put in, the blood that goes into each of their cases, all for less money than most lawyers make.

Prosecutor Emily Hernandez brings me to yet another particular love of mine: unexpected pregnancies. It happens to a lot of women—it even happened to me. And I love being able to take the frightening and unplanned, and turn it into a well of never-ending love, as the birth of my daughter did for me. Added to that, Emily's in her forties, and the father of her child...well, he's a Colton. You can see why she stepped out of her ordered, controlled world to fall into bed with him. And why, when she thought it was only a fling, she didn't worry about him being ten years younger than her. But...making a family with him? Not in the plan at all.

Tara Taylor

PROTECTING COLTON'S BABY

Tara Taylor Quinn

Special thanks and acknowledgment are given to
Tara Taylor Quinn for her contribution to
The Coltons of New York miniseries.

Recycling programs
for this product may
not exist in your area.

ISBN-13: 978-1-335-73826-4

Protecting Colton's Baby

Copyright © 2023 by Harlequin Enterprises ULC

For questions and comments about the quality of this book, please contact us at CustomerService@Harlequin.com.

Harlequin Enterprises ULC
22 Adelaide St. West, 41st Floor
Toronto, Ontario M5H 4E3, Canada
www.Harlequin.com

Printed in U.S.A.

A *USA TODAY* bestselling author of over a hundred novels in twenty languages, **Tara Taylor Quinn** has sold more than seven million copies. Known for her intense emotional fiction, Ms. Quinn's novels have received critical acclaim in the UK and most recently from Harvard. She is the recipient of the Reader's Choice Award, and has appeared often on local and national TV, including *CBS Sunday Morning*.

For TTQ offers, news and contests, visit www.tarataylorquinn.com!

Books by Tara Taylor Quinn

Harlequin Romantic Suspense

The Coltons of New York

Protecting Colton's Baby

Sierra's Web

Tracking His Secret Child

The Coltons of Colorado

Colton Countdown

Where Secrets are Safe

Her Detective's Secret Intent
Shielded in the Shadows
Falling for His Suspect

The Coltons of Grave Gulch

Colton's Killer Pursuit

Visit the Author Profile page at Harlequin.com for more titles.

For Rachel Marie, you've been my inspiration since the day you were born. It never ends. Nor does my love for you. Be happy, Baby Girl.

Chapter 1

A forty-three-year-old woman did not belong in front of the shelf of home pregnancy tests.

She just didn't.

Assistant District Attorney Emily Hernandez had made a solid career out of getting facts right.

Statistics said that hormones to fight bone density were in her future, not supplements that would stabilize and facilitate a healthy fetus.

When a young mother with a toddler in tow entered the aisle, Emily had to step forward to let her pass. The plump-legged little girl attached to her mother through tightly clasped hands said something completely unintelligible. Or so Emily thought, until the mother responded with an enthusiastic, "I know!"

At which point Emily was certain they were commenting on the absurdity of the prosecutor showing such age standing, well, where she was standing. Maybe thinking she was contemplating a purchase for her daughter?

How embarrassing.

Her daughter. If she was…she wasn't…but if she was…would it be a girl?

She wasn't.

Should she buy the white box with pink lettering? The purple with white letters? Or the blue? Hands at her sides, she wasn't ready to touch any of them. To be seen touching them.

Dear God, she was going to have to walk up to the register and pay for it.

Bad idea, visiting a drugstore so close to her office. And to the courthouse. Any judge she appeared before, any attorney she argued against, could walk in. See her.

Gulping, she glanced around to make certain she had the aisle to herself. What if someone from her own office saw her?

Turning, she stepped quickly into the next aisle. Took some deep breaths to calm down. Focused on potato chips and other bagged snacks. But she couldn't contemplate buying any. Not until she knew for sure that she wasn't pregnant…

Just get the damned thing.

With anxiety threatening to overtake her, Emily strode back around the corner, picked the first box her hand touched—purple with white lettering—and looked straight ahead as she took it to the register.

She had to know.

A practical woman would take care of the situation by finding out the facts. And she was the most practical woman she knew.

There was no line at the register. Speeding up before

someone could round a corner and get ahead of her, she stared at a candy display as she put the box on the counter. She'd never seen the cashier before in her life. Within seconds the box and all the things it hinted at were encased inside a plastic Duane Reade pharmacy bag, covered by the chocolate bar she'd thrown on top of it, and further buried within the satchel that served as her purse.

She had a challenging caseload awaiting her. Had to get the test behind her so she could give her career—which pretty much encompassed the entirety of her daily life—her complete focus.

And she had to do it without anyone, not even the hot dog vendor on the corner, ever knowing that there was even a slight hint of a possibility that she could have a child growing inside her.

Frigid February air hit her as she pushed through the door, freezing her skin and her feelings. Pulling her long black coat tighter with the belt at the waist, she barreled forward. Of course, the light would turn green as soon as she hit the corner. Hunching a bit against the chill, she awaited her turn to cross, wanting to chuckle over the absurdity of her little errand.

Fear stifled every ounce of lightness from her soul. She couldn't be pregnant. Other than one ending-in-disaster engagement two decades before, she'd never even been in a serious relationship. The no-strings-attached liaison she'd had with Cormac Colton—a stupendous PI, gorgeous, but also so much younger than her that he'd still been filled with that vibrant belief that he could change the world—had not ended well.

One week with her and he'd abruptly said he was done.

There'd been no conversation. No explanation. Not even a casual "see ya around." He'd been out.

Finished with her.

She could not be carrying his child. Shivering with cold, and dread, she saw traffic slowing. She stood up straight, ready to cross over toward her office, and lost all air as a thump against her back and around her shoulder shoved her off balance, and, locking her in a deathly grasp, a body propelled her to the opened door of a black SUV.

"What!" she hollered, shoving against the force trying to take over her body. The satchel hanging crossways on her body didn't help her any, but she didn't let it slow her down. With a kick and a screamed demand to "Stop," she slapped out at her attacker, catching the side of his head with a whack. People surrounded them.

There'd be a pool of witnesses.

And in spite of her blows and all the onlookers, her abductor shoved her off the curb and, with a hand on her head, was still trying to force her down into the vehicle.

"No!" She screamed again, rearing back, bracing herself against the outside of the SUV. The big gloved hand at her head pushed harder and her forehead hit the doorjamb just as she stomped on the man's foot.

And...

Then she was free. Her accoster was hauled off her and she stepped back up on the curb, half gasping, half sobbing, feeling surrounded by a wall of gaping bystanders as she heard the assailant's "I'll get you next time."The man who'd grabbed her dove into the back seat of the SUV, which sped off, leaving her staring at her rescuer's wide shoulders and dark hair.

Dark hair that seemed professionally mussed. With a wayward spike of hair to the left of his collar. She saw the hardly noticeable little strand as the man turned.

No.

She was hallucinating.

Had lost her mind in the fray.

She gripped her bag to her side, still shaking, vaguely aware, in the mere seconds that had passed, that multiple voices were speaking to her.

She only heard the words from one.

"Emily, did he hurt you?"

She noted the worry. Stared.

"Call the police," the man shouted as he stood inches from Emily, his dark eyes filled with a concern that touched her far more deeply than her abductor had done.

"Already done," another male voice said.

"And an ambulance," her rescuer continued. For a man barely in his thirties, Cormac Colton had a boatload of confidence and authority in his tone.

Cormac. He was really there. Not just a figment of her way too harried state of mind. "I don't need an ambulance," she said then, finding her own stash of commanding tone, as the light changed again and she stepped off the curb to cross the street.

"Emily." He reached for her shoulder, not with force, but in an attempt to keep her there. "You need to talk to the police."

"Send them to my office. ADA Emily Hernandez," she announced to the crowd in general, and, turning her back, hurried into the crosswalk before the light could change. If the cops didn't show up, she could call them from the phone on her desk.

Arriving at the other side of the street, she stepped up onto the sidewalk, with Cormac right there beside her.

"I'm fine, you can go." She gave him as much of a dismissive tone as she could muster, shaking harder.

Someone had just tried to kidnap her!

And the man who'd dumped her had suddenly shown up out of thin air to save her?

Her satchel…the box… Cormac Colton crowding her space…she hugged her bag with both hands, holding it close.

"I'm coming with you," the far-too-memorable voice said beside her. "I'll need to give my statement to the police as well."

As good as she was at coming up with logical arguments, she came up blank. Because of the bump to her head? She reached her hand up, but the skin was hardly tender enough to warrant a bruise.

The best sex she'd ever had was accompanying her to her office, where a pregnancy test would be sitting in her satchel, and police officers would be waiting for her victim statement.

She'd almost been kidnapped! Who wanted her? And for what? She tried to focus on recent cases, threats made or perps she'd put away getting released, but came up completely blank on all of it.

Cold and breathless, she wanted to cry.

And silently cursed her luck instead.

What in the hell had she done to deserve such cruel twists of fate?

Adrenaline pumping, Cormac kept pace next to the feisty prosecutor, keeping his body as close to her as he could without actually touching her again.

He was not allowed to touch her. Not unless it was a life-and-death situation. Her life.

His rule. Issued firmly to himself two months before when he'd broken off his liaison with her.

She didn't speak.

He focused on everything and everyone around them. Shielding her from behind, watching what was ahead, even once they were inside the DA building and heading to her office. It didn't matter to him if either of them knew the people they passed. Until they figured out why someone had just tried to force her into a vehicle, everyone was suspect.

She made a beeline behind her desk, still clutching the big purse she wore, but didn't sit down. "You stalking me?" Her tone was challenging, not scared.

Cormac's head turned, his gaze swinging toward the door he'd just come through, only to find that no one was there. Turning back, he saw her staring at him with an air of "how dare you" about her. "You're talking to *me*?" Shaking his head, he started to feel like he was in some kind of bizarre nightmare.

First, the near kidnapping, and now this?

Yeah, he'd been kind of dreading seeing her again—for a few reasons—but…

"Yes. How else do you explain turning up in the exact moment I'm the target of a kidnapping? If that's what it was. If you think this is some kind of joke…"

"Emily!" He raised his voice enough to get her attention. He figured shock was getting to her.

She blinked, didn't take her question back.

"Of course, I'm not stalking you," he told her.

"You could be. With your stellar PI skills, how would I know?"

Mouth gaping, he stared. Was she for real?

"You seriously think I'd stalk you?" He couldn't even compute that one.

With a visibly deep breath, she sank to her chair, her purse on her lap. She was still clutching it with both hands. "No, of course not."

She looked back up at him. "But you have to admit, it's odd that just when someone tries to accost me, you're suddenly right there…"

"What we need to be talking about is who's out to get you," he said then, coming closer, but only to sink into the chair across from her desk. One they'd stupidly, stupendously, had sex in. He had to sit so he didn't keep staring at the damned thing.

Where in the hell were the police? He grabbed his phone, intending to call one of his relatives to find out who was on duty in the area, but the look in her eyes stopped him.

A mixture of authority—and fear. Almost to the point of self-doubt. Emily was one of the most confident women he'd ever met. Which had been part of the incredible turn-on…

"I need to know why you were there," she said then.

Eager to help where he could, he sat forward, elbows on the arms of the chair. "I was on my way to see you," he told her. "To ask you about the case Humphrey Kelly was about to testify on when he went missing. You were the ADA…"

The seeming relief that flashed across her expression was confusing, too. Why else would he have been there? Had she really thought he'd been watching her? The idea was ludicrous. He was the one who'd broken off things between them.

Cut them off at the quick, was more like it.

To the point of rudeness.

And…she had to be grasping at straws. Trying to find a reason for the events that had just transpired. She must be scared out of her wits. It was the only explanation that made sense out of her making more of his sudden appearance than the kidnapping he'd thwarted.

You'd think she'd be grateful to him.

Thanking God he'd been there.

"I've already been asked about that case three times," she told him. "He's a psychiatrist, was scheduled to give expert witness testimony that we didn't really need to get a conviction, and he didn't show up. That's all I know."

Humphrey was so much more. But he'd get to that. At the moment they had to figure out what had just happened, who wanted her and for what. They needed to secure her safety until they found out.

He'd been about to tell her so, when two uniformed officers he didn't know showed up at the door of her office.

And, glad to have them there, ready to work toward Emily's well-being, he put his own concern on the back burner while they did their job.

Chapter 2

The officers took thorough reports. They suggested that Emily not walk along the streets any more than was necessary while they looked into things, warning her to stay away from the curb, to try to walk in the middle of throngs rather than alone, and close enough to buildings to duck inside if need be. But not close to alleys or doorways where someone could haul her inside.

Basically, they scared the heck out of her.

Their departure was a relief, more so because she expected Cormac Colton to go with them. She'd already given him the little she knew about the Humphrey Kelly disappearance. Cormac's brother was a detective. He had a sister who was a cop. And they had other family who were members of the NYPD network. They didn't need her.

And...she'd be in good hands.

So that was one good thing about the day.

About him.

Except that, as the officers left, even as Cormac took a few steps outside her door with them, he didn't actually go. Instead, after those couple of yards had enlarged the distance between him and her, he spun around and came back.

Filling her with cold and dread.

She couldn't help him. Even if she knew more about Humphrey than she realized, she'd have to deal with someone else. The detective on the case. Not the hired PI. She and Cormac Colton could absolutely not work together again.

She'd point-blank refuse if she had to.

If it came to that.

If he forced the issue.

"I'm fine now," she told him as he reentered the room. "You don't have to hang around."

"You were just…"

A wave of her hand, a strong shake of her head, cut him off. "Getting threatened is a job hazard," she blurted out. And then more words tumbled out on top of those. "I get threatening emails and phone calls, too. Mostly untraceable. I'm used to them."

She couldn't let him see her fear.

He'd once told her they were perfect for each other. Then he'd ghosted her.

And now she needed him to get the hell out. She had to pee on a stick and prove to herself that she wasn't pregnant so she could quit acting like a complete ninny and get busy with figuring out who'd tried to haul her off. She needed to concentrate and remember a smell, a ring or scar, anything familiar. Because as the police had questioned her, she'd had nothing.

Except the faces of potential witnesses.

And the man who'd ultimately been in exactly the right place at the right time, and saved her from God knew what…

He was standing there, watching her.

He'd risked his life for her.

"I didn't even thank you," she said, her tone softening. "You possibly just saved my life." Chills of horror, of fear—and of supreme gratitude—passed through her as she stared at him.

Then, when he shrugged and gave her that warm "we've got a thing" look, she immediately broke eye contact with him. Fidgeted.

Inadvertently kicked the satchel she'd dropped to the floor at some point during their interviews with the police officers.

And remembered the purple box.

Now she felt no gratitude at all toward the man who, two months before, had been a partner to one of her current scares. Potentially a life-altering one. How dare he sit there and smile kindly at her like their little fling was a fond memory and nothing more?

"Dare I hope I won enough good favor, maybe added to the fact that we know each other, to trade for a bit more detail on the case Humphrey Kelly was testifying on the day he disappeared? He was at the courthouse. Disappeared right before he was due to testify. It just seems logical that there's some connection. Anything you can tell me, however inconsequential you might think it to be, might help."

"I have nothing else to give you," she told him, refusing to let Cormac see any chinks in her armor. "He was simply going to testify that the accused was of sound mind.

That's it. The testimony was merely a formality. Just a statement for the record."

"Please, Emily." His gaze bore into her, as though he could, with just a look, compel her to give him whatever he wanted.

Because, for a short time, he'd been able to do just that? Because she'd wanted their sexual encounters as badly as he had...

"While I am officially working the Kelly disappearance as part of the team my brother put together, this is far more than a case to us. Humphrey Kelly is like an uncle to me. He's not biologically related, but he pretty much raised me after my dad died when I was fourteen."

Her heart lurched. She hadn't known he'd been that young when his father died. Hadn't had time to ask, due to the amount of time they'd spent in bed together during the one week that their *thing* had lasted.

She couldn't let him suck her in again. Every second he was there agitated her more. "I've told you what I know." She was sorry if she sounded harsh, but she needed him gone.

"There's got to be something more." Cormac didn't relent. Or seem to get the hint that he'd overstayed his welcome. "Was there a reason someone wanted the defendant to appear less than stable? Who'd have stood to gain from such a ruling?"

"The defendant is Evan Smith. He's on trial for shooting to death three people after a barfight. That's all public knowledge, so you obviously already have it. Dr. Kelly's testimony was merely a formality and that's all I know about his involvement. Dotting i's and crossing t's. You're the guy who has a passion for the truth," she shot at him as pressure built inside her. "How can you expect me to come up with facts I don't have?"

How could anyone expect her to confront the facts she did have, without knowing all the facts? What did it mean that Cormac Colton was standing in her office, having just probably saved her life, while she was sitting with her calf resting against the satchel that held the test that was going to give her the one fact she needed most at the moment?

She needed it even more than knowing who'd just attempted to kidnap her.

Was she pregnant? Had her life changed on a dime? She was forty-three years old! She couldn't be a new mom.

Had whoever was after her just threatened the life of her child, too?

Had karma brought Cormac to the rescue just in time?

To save his own child?

Panic rode over all sense of logic, leaving her in a haze of truths and questions and fear, while the man who'd upended her life stood there watching it all.

"You hate deception, Cormac," she said with anger coming forth as her defense, filling her voice with accusation. "Yet now you want me to come up with some magical piece of evidence that isn't there?"

Pulling back, as though shocked, he opened his mouth, but she didn't give him a chance to speak—to confuse her more.

"Speaking of which," she blew out at him, "didn't you deceive me just a little when you led me to believe that our liaison was mutually beneficial in a long-term sense, since we'd discovered that we were both adamantly against anything more than great friends with benefits when schedules fell in line? And then just one week in, just a few weeks before Christmas, you abruptly cut me off, as though you'd suddenly discovered I was a murderer or something... treating me like little more than..." She stopped, midsentence. Hearing herself.

Horrified with herself.

All the problems she was facing that morning, and she was going to bring *that* up?

The man might be equally to blame for the cause of the stark panic that had driven her steps to the store that morning, but...he didn't know.

And...if she was...he'd have to know.

The thought choked all other words from her throat.

Cormac steeled his emotions as the most vibrant, sexy woman he'd ever known seemed to be falling apart in from of him.

Needing him, even if she didn't realize it.

As strong and capable as she absolutely was, she'd almost been abducted less than an hour before, would have been hauled away if he hadn't been able to intervene at the last second. But for a moment there, she'd lost all say over her life, as, in spite of her fighting back, her kidnapper had succeeded in taking control of her.

Cormac was being an ass, completely unlike himself, trying to make his search for Humphrey more important than the trauma she'd just suffered. His uncle's life was vital. But so was hers.

Nor was he going to be able to pretend seeing her again hadn't hit him. Hard. Try as he might, no way he was going to be able to just walk away again. Not until he knew she was out of danger.

"Things aren't always what they seem," he said, with

the intensity simmering between them lacing his tone, as well.

She'd accused him of being duplicitous in starting a long-term relationship with her and then just cutting it off.

Truth stung.

But what would she have had him do? Tell her that he'd broken his own rules, her rules, too, their rules, by starting to fall for her as more than a no-strings-attached liaison? Like some kid panting over a real woman.

Which was probably what she'd have thought him, faulting his youth to her eleven years more of experience for his lack of ability to follow through on their agreement to keep things casual.

And even if she hadn't, it wouldn't have mattered. He was most definitely not losing himself to the vagaries of emotion that blinded him to truth, that led to lost lives, a second time in his life. One dead lover was enough.

"I'm going to need a list of possible suspects," he said then, his tone brooking no refusal, continuing with, "Threats you've received, anonymous and otherwise, anyone who might want to hurt you, all the cases you've worked on, no matter how far back, since someone you put away, someone bearing a grudge, might have recently been released from prison…"

He broke off as all expression left her face. He'd gone too far. Too fast. But…

"I don't need your help."

He could see how she'd feel that way. But he couldn't just walk out on her. All het up, fueled by adrenaline, and something more he couldn't name, he was a little brutal in his delivery of the truth. "You're in danger, Emily. Real danger. With no idea where it's coming from or when or how it'll be back. And finding dangerous guys who know how to get lost is what I do. You know I'm good at it." They'd met working a case together. "You seriously want me to just walk out of here and leave you with no answers? You want to have to walk in the middle of the sidewalk, finding crowds to get lost in, to be afraid of what might be just behind you, or waiting in a doorway to get a second chance at you? I can see the fear emanating off you..."

With both hands on her desk, she stood, facing him, visibly trembling, and said, "You want to know the greatest source of my fear, Cormac?"

"Absolutely." He'd go head-to-head with her on that one.

She didn't stand up to him even for a second, perplexing him with the ease of her capitulation, until he realized she was reaching for something. On the floor, by her feet.

Was she about to pull a gun on him and order him out?

He knew the thought was ludicrous. It had no merit, but he couldn't figure out...

She had a box in her hand. Cutesy purple with white lettering. He didn't get it.

Until...he did.

Then he didn't know what to do. Couldn't find a single coherent thought.

Except...they were encapsulated by a swarm of current, unidentified, life-threatening danger and she'd just dropped a pregnancy test on the desk between them.

"We used protection."

On the verge of flying off the handle propelled by the myriad emotions coursing through her, Emily took his words to be his way of asking if he was the father.

Ready to blast him for the insult—she wouldn't be sharing the news with him if he wasn't—she took one look at the whiteness around his lips, the blank look in his usually compelling dark eyes, and said, "I know. And listen, really, even if it failed, at my age, there's little chance that I'd actually get pregnant from one instance of escaped biological product. More likely, I'm going through the change of life early, getting sporadic with my cycle. I just started to wonder 'what if' to the point of interfering with my normal focus and had to make sure. If you hadn't been standing here trying to pressure me at a time when I'm already feeling about as much pressure as I can take, you wouldn't ever even have known…"

She watched him. And just kept babbling. Until his gaze homed in on her in that way he had of making her feel like she was the only thing he saw. Then her words stilled midstream.

"You're late?" It was like he was leaning over the desk, instead of standing in front of it. Cupping her face with his hand rather than clutching the edge of her desk with white-knuckled fingers.

She nodded. There was no condemnation. Or anger.

"You ever been late before?"

Not a whole two months. Not even six weeks. She shook her head.

"Then let's go take the test."

"Cormac…"

"Seriously," he said, standing, his arms folded against the muscled chest that still appeared in her dreams. Or in her mind's eye at inconvenient times during the day. "This is huge. For both of us. We need to know. Now. Let's do this."

If she hadn't been so worked up, she might have smiled.

Her decade-plus younger lover had been so vibrant, still believing that he could change huge portions of the world just by needing it so. That intensity had been part of what had drawn her to him—and, for a brief time, she'd felt that she was that young again. Or at least, had experienced reinstilled belief that her work, her life, made a real difference…

Licking her lips, she nodded toward the box on her desk. "The test…it's not an 'us' thing, Cormac. I do it alone."

With a shrug, he picked up the box. "I meant, let's get the results," he said, as he handed it to her. "We need to know if an attempted kidnapping, on top of Humphrey's kidnapping—which could make it two people from the same case going missing, by the way—is all we're dealing with."

She took the box. There was no other logical choice. And slipped into the small, private half bath attached to her office, hoping she wasn't so bothered by him just outside the door that she developed a shy bladder and couldn't pee.

Chapter 3

Her bladder wasn't shy.

"You coming out?" Cormac called, so close to the door she imagined it vibrated with his energy.

Standing there holding the plastic handle, shaking now that knowing her future fate was imminent, she called back, "It takes three minutes to register results."

"Waiting is the part we can do together." She heard a brush against the door, like he was leaning against it. Or ready to join her inside the room.

He wouldn't. She knew him well enough to know that he'd respect a closed door. But the answer she waited for was equally important to him.

Device in hand, held flat, she opened the door. He wasn't noticing her at all. And he was making her more nervous when she'd thought it wasn't possible to be any more ready to explode. "Don't stare at it."

He glanced up at her, assessing her face, and she almost told him to go ahead and stare at the plastic test stick. But she stared back at him, instead.

If she was pregnant…her child was his, too.

For the two weeks she'd been in denial, and then all the time she'd spent working herself up to the point of testing, she'd been thinking in terms of her. Her life. Mammoth changes.

Cormac Colton had walked out. Making it clear he was done with her. She'd never made it to the part where he'd be affected, too, by the world-changing accident.

Not as much as she would, of course. He could walk away. She couldn't.

"What's a plus mean?"

Her gaze shot to the apparatus in her hand the second she heard his words. The plus sign in the screen was unmistakable. Clear as day. Not even a little bit faint.

And then, as her hand shook uncontrollably, the weighty piece of plastic was taken away. Cormac set it on the desk.

"Positive. It means positive," he said, his tone far-off and unfamiliar to her.

Positive.

She was pregnant. Sinking down to the chair in front of her desk, she stared at the piece of plastic before her. Her stomach roiling with emotion, she thought for a second there she was going to be sick, but something completely unexpected nestled within the madness swirling inside her: surreal elation.

Yeah. There it was. Who'd have thought…

"I'm going to have a baby." And she wasn't completely devastated by the thought. In fact, the preparation she'd been busy doing—getting herself ready to know that she'd never ever have a child, even though she'd men-

tally taken the possibility off her table years before—
slipped away unneeded.

Filled with an entirely new kind of energy, feeling like
she didn't know herself at all, she grabbed the stick, suf-
fused with the same kind of single-minded determina-
tion that had built her successful career.

"I can do this." She didn't know how. She stood
through a wave of terror as she thought about buying
baby stuff, and then, looking straight at Cormac, said,
"I can do this."

Alone. Just as she always did pretty much everything.
Made her decisions, bought her apartment, paid her bills,
built her career, cooked her dinners, decorated and…
and…she'd learn the rest.

She was a good learner. A quick learner.

Her parents, retired to Florida, would teach her how.
They'd been great at it.

Her parents…

"You're pregnant." Cormac's tone wasn't quite a question, but it had none of his usual note of confidence. She
stared up at him, standing between the desk and the bathroom door with his fingers pulling at the collar of the
pullover he'd had on under his coat.

"Yeah." She hadn't really comprehended the idea, either.

"We should get married. The courthouse is just a
block away. We can file for a license now and appear
before the judge tomorrow. My older brother, Sean, he
just got engaged and he's looking into things like that.
He told me. Twenty-four hours is the wait time."

Cormac didn't want to marry her. He'd dropped her
like a hot potato. She was eleven years older than him.
Had more wrinkles than he did.

He wasn't serious. He was just in shock. Reacting. And her treacherous heart, leaping as it had, needed to get itself in check. A conversation she'd be having with it forthwith.

"I'll never marry a man who doesn't love me," she said. And then, hating the needy sound of that, added, just as succinctly, "A man I don't love."

His nod was immediate. Confirming her belief that he hadn't meant the proposal.

Almost to the point of insulting.

"Let's sleep on the idea and reconvene on it later," he added several seconds too late.

"Sounds good. I'll call you tomorrow."

Right. That's what she was going to do. But she was glad to have the conversation over so quickly. And if, a small, small, tiny, minute part of her was disappointed that he didn't seem even the least bit happy, she didn't give it enough notice to matter.

After all, she was old enough to know better.

He'd been dismissed.

Truthfully, one part of him wanted out of there probably more than she wanted him gone.

Stunned, he stood there with one clear goal. He could not leave her.

The woman had gotten under his skin a couple of months before, in a way no other woman had, which was why he'd broken things off with her so abruptly. Because he absolutely would not ever again be in a relationship where emotion was the prime component keeping him there.

But she'd nearly been abducted.

And now, she was carrying his kid? No way he could walk out on that.

"Sleeping on things, talking tomorrow, that's all good," he said, hating his seeming lack of control over anything in that moment. "But there's this morning's event—"

"I'll be fine," she interrupted.

"You were almost kidnapped," he continued, and held up his hand as he said, "and before you tell me again that threats come with the job, I know damned well that abduction is not a part of your average business day. Beyond that, had you been taken, had your life been in danger, my kid's life would have been, too."

He gave her a chance to argue that, meeting her gaze. Almost daring her to tell him he was wrong.

Her silence spurred more words from him, things he was making up as he went along. "I think that at least until the police, and I, have a chance to investigate this morning's incident, you should stay with me. It's not like you've never been to my place. You know there's space there for you…"

They'd had sex on the bed in his spare room.

"You know how easy it is for you to catch a cab to work from there, but we'll need to talk about you coming to the office at all, until this guy is caught…"

She wasn't immediately jumping down his throat. Which scared him.

And satisfied him a little, too.

"You're a bit more vulnerable, now that we know you're pregnant." He pushed home his advantage. "And as the father, I have a responsibility to the kid as well. Your staying at my place allows me to take care of all sides of the situation to the best of my ability."

She might think, as she'd once said, her decade on him gave her wisdom he'd yet to gain, but he didn't buy that for a second.

He had no idea how it was going to work, her actually staying at his place rather than visiting for hot and heavy sexual encounters, no idea how he'd be with a woman in his private domain for more than sex—most particularly her. Didn't even want to think about her naked in the shower, sleeping down the hall or even eating dinner at his table, for that matter. But he didn't take back the offer.

Wouldn't even consider doing so.

It spoke to his shocked state that it took him a moment to realize she wasn't saying no.

"No one would think to look for you there," he said softly. No one but the two of them had any knowledge of what had transpired between them. Not only had it been extremely short-lived, but they'd both gone out of their way to make sure that they weren't seen together.

They'd met working on a case. Neither of them had wanted anyone to think them less than professional or fully committed to their careers.

More than that, they'd made sure that no one ever had a chance to think that there was more to their association than would ever be there.

A shared kid kind of threw that all to hell.

And mattered not at all in the moment. He had to convince her to go home with him, to give him a chance to figure out who'd tried to kidnap her, and to keep her—and the kid—safe in the meanwhile.

"Please, Emily." Begging wasn't beneath him apparently.

And worth every ego-killing second he stood there waiting when she finally nodded.

With her life her work, and her retired parents her only family, Emily stood in her office, trembling, realizing that other than people she was friendly with at work, she was completely alone in the city. With someone after her and a baby to protect.

Giving in to Cormac's request that she stay with him seemed the best choice. She wasn't letting her guard down. The man was all enthusiasm and great talk one minute, and then gone the next, but until she had a chance to assimilate the morning's events, to let the police—or Cormac if he really intended to help—find her accoster, she saw nothing wrong in allowing a father to protect his kid. The fact that the child resided inside her body made her presence with the two of them a basic necessity.

But…

"It has to be understood that the liaison that ended between us is still over," she said, reminding herself of the cutthroat way he'd walked out of her life. "There is absolutely nothing between us except the child."

Child sounded so much more distant in her head, less intimate. Hearing herself say the word aloud, not so much so.

She couldn't believe she was going to be a mother.

A replay of the attempted kidnapping flashed across her mind, and fear—new and much sharper—sliced through her. The baby…she might never have become a mother. Her little one might never have known life.

"You said something about wanting access to my cases, to people I've prosecuted who were recently released from prison and…other things," she said, as that near abduction loomed, squeezing air out of her lungs anew. Turning, she spread her arm to sweep across her desk. "It's all yours. And, actually, I can access most of it from my laptop. It's secure, I go online through my phone, also secure, so I can work from home. Or…other…places."

On high speed suddenly, filled with panic-laced octane, she gathered up the few hard copy files she needed, her laptop, a legal pad and a pen, all of which she shoved into her satchel, and turned toward the door.

Cormac, to his credit, didn't say a word.

He just waited while she did what she had to do, and then followed her out.

Cormac took his cues from Emily, giving her all the space he could, until she announced that she'd need to stop by her place on the way to his. No way he could let that happen.

"We have to assume that whoever is out to get you knows where you live," he pointed out, in spite of the fact that he knew he was likely scaring her.

She needed to feel afraid. In her situation, a good dose of fear would go a long way toward keeping her safe.

But he wasn't totally without empathy. "I'm calling a cab to pick us up outside the secure entrance," he told her as he ushered her down the empty stairwell rather than heading toward the elevator she'd intended to use. "Make a list of whatever you need and where to find it and I'll send my sister, Eva, to pick it up. She's always up for any favor I ask, and I am for her, too. She's in uniform, a noob, but fearless, in case anyone's lying in wait. And if someone is watching your place, he'll see her uniform and know the police are watching it, too, watching for him."

"You never said you were close with your sister."

There were a lot of things he hadn't told her. Some genetic...he paled. "I also never told you I'm a twin," he dropped as lightly as he could. "Not identical, though, so I don't think that's a thing here."

Two sacs, not one, so hopefully not genetic. But it

wasn't like he really knew beans about twins that ran in families, one way or the other.

She'd stopped on the stairs, one up from him, mouth open, staring. It was hard to believe that the fit, lusciously curvaceous body with the dark wavy hair tumbling around it, that the determined woman who so confidently owned it, was pregnant with his baby.

"You're a twin."

"Yeah, but, like I said, not identical."

"Brother or sister?"

"Brother. His name's Liam."

"Is he local?" With her standing up there looking down on him, he felt compelled to answer.

"Yeah. We're all working the Humphrey Kelly case together. My brother Sean, the detective—" he'd told her about Sean during the casework that had brought Cormac and Emily together in the first place, but she'd already known him "—Eva, Liam and I."

"Liam's a cop, too?"

"No, he's a stupidly rich dude who runs an awareness program for the precinct." He was also an ex-con but that was a story for another less stressful, probably-never-going-to-happen day. Unless she needed to know due to the kid.

He turned to head down and heard her voice behind him.

"We were together seven nights in a row and you never thought to tell me you're a twin?"

She hadn't budged. So maybe the genetic thing was an issue, still. Or, she was just freaking out because it was a freaking out kind of day.

"I didn't tell you I had a sister who was a rookie cop, either."

"Yes, you did. The night you saw a missed call from her and then when you called her back, she didn't pick up."

Yeah. Eva had been on duty. He'd panicked for a second. Until Eva had texted that she'd get with him later. He'd forgotten about it the second Emily's lips had touched his.

"You weren't used to her being on the streets yet," the ADA reminded him as they continued down the stairs.

And he was reminded of just how good she was at remembering every detail about everything—and drawing concrete conclusions from the mix. It made her great at her job.

It had also made her a compelling and unforgettable companion. Emily Hernandez, unlike most women he'd spent time with, stimulated him, captivated him as much mentally as she did physically. Which was why he'd had to run, not walk, out her door and not look back.

And while he was going to keep her firmly in his sights until he knew she was safe, he still wasn't looking back. With a baby on the way, him keeping his heart free from the kind of emotional entanglement that blinded him was now more critical than ever.

Chapter 4

Eva Colton wasn't the one who brought Emily's things. Emily had been hoping to meet the young woman who'd followed her brothers into law enforcement.

Instead, as she stood in the spacious living area of Cormac's apartment, clutching the satchel hanging from her shoulder, trying to pretend she hadn't had sex on the couch just feet away from her, she watched him open his door to a Colton she did know, Cormac's older brother, Sean.

"Detective Colton," she said, stepping forward, reaching out her hand for a shake, needing to assert control over the situation before she lost any hope of gaining any. That was before she realized he wasn't just there to see Cormac on business.

She didn't notice the duffel he'd had slung on his back until it slid forward as he reached for her hand. Instead of giving her a brusque shake, he slid the strap of the gym bag–looking carryall down his arm and handed it to her. "Eva asked that I give this to you."

So much for being the professional in control. Now they all knew she was staying with their brother. How embarrassing.

And…how to explain…

"Cormac told me that he gave you little choice but to use his guest room until we get some things sorted out," Sean continued, seemingly having no trouble commandeering all of the control she'd been hoping to obtain. "I apologize for my brother's heavy-handedness in this matter and want you to know that if you'd rather be in a hotel or someplace else, we can assign an officer to keep you company. At least until we get an initial look at things…"

"I told Sean that I, um, insisted that you stay here, so that I can provide you with protection, and also work with you to figure out who's after you. Since, you know, your abduction follows so closely behind Humphrey going missing, both in or near the courthouse, and with both of you associated with the same case…"

He hadn't told his brother she was pregnant with his child, Emily translated the slightly awkward, completely unlike Cormac, explanation.

She nodded. Looked Sean Colton in the eye, and said, "I'd just as soon stay here, if you don't mind. I wouldn't be here now if I didn't agree that it was a good idea. I want this settled as soon as possible, and intend to be as involved as possible in figuring out what happened this morning and why." Then she tacked on, "In case Cormac didn't tell you, I'm paying your brother for his protection. I worked with him on a case a couple of months back and have hired him to work for me on this matter."

Cormac's gaze shot to her. She read the argument there but didn't think he'd call her out in front of his brother. And she didn't budge from her stance. She'd come up with the idea of having Cormac officially work her case during the drive over from the courthouse. To keep things clean and tidy between them. She just hadn't mentioned her plan to him. But now it was official.

He'd argue when they were alone. And she'd offer to leave. She held the trump card in that particular matter.

And she needed not to feel as though her pregnancy made her dependent on him.

"He didn't mention the money, no," Sean said, sliding a glance toward Cormac, who, taking her bag, headed toward the hall leading back to the bedrooms.

"We hadn't decided on terms when I spoke to you," Cormac said over his shoulder.

The way he'd taken her bag, brooking no argument, she knew she'd pissed him off, making him look bad in front of his brother. And acknowledged, silently, that she probably could have found a better way to handle the situation.

"I'm here to let you know that I'm the detective who's been assigned to your attempted abduction case," Sean said, moving toward the far end of the room, just off the kitchen, to take a seat at Cormac's dining table.

Oh. "Does Cormac know?" she asked, as the father of her child came back out to join them.

"I did know, yes," he said then, his tone challenging as he looked at her. "Sean texted to say he was on his way over."

Okay, fine. Neither one of them was doing so well in the trusting each other with communication department.

She flashed Cormac a glance, nodded, and looked with equal gratitude and acceptance as she pulled her laptop out of her satchel and said, "I can send each of you a list of my current cases right now. It'll take a little bit of time to research recent prison releases and to gather up previous cases that would be more likely to have been involved, but I'll get on that right away."

Both men nodded, and Sean said, "I wanted to let both of you know that we got a license plate number on the SUV from witness statements and have already talked to the driver. He's employed by a private car service and was dispatched to a corner just a block from the courthouse to pick up a Tom Jones. That name mean anything to you?"

A slice of fear shot through her as Sean Cormac's intent gaze focused on her. The near kidnapping…it had been real. Attached to a man with a name.

Frantically searching her memory banks, she shook her head slowly. Then turned back to her computer, and with fingers fumbling on the keyboard, ran a quick document search.

"I come up with Jones. And with Tom. But not together," she told both men.

"It's likely not the guy's real name," Cormac told her, his tone more sympathetic than anything. Soothing her in the way he'd had from the first day she'd met him.

Emily wasn't, and never had been, a woman who needed soothing.

Finding her gaze holding on to the man for too long, she quickly glanced back at her screen and then over to Cormac's brother. If Sean had noticed anything passing between the two of them, he was professional enough not to acknowledge it. Instead, he said, "Jones told the driver that his sister had gone off her meds, that she was out of her head and a friend of hers had called him and told him that she was headed to the courthouse to insist on seeing the judge who'd ordered her remanded to a mental health facility. He warned the driver that there was a possibility she'd resist being picked up."

"Where was the driver supposed to take them?"

Sean named a professional building not far from the courthouse. "Jones said that his sister's psychiatrist had offices in the building. We've got a basic sketch of the guy, but not much from surveillance footage so far. With the winter coat, it's hard to tell his build, and the hood he was wearing along with the scarf concealed his features."

She'd never even seen the man's face. Only the black leather of his coat in the arm around her, black gloves and shoes.

"Officers are going around the building now with a description and the sketch," Sean continued.

"And when the pickup went askew?" she asked, shuddering in spite of her attempt not to do so.

"The driver said Jones apologized, asked to be dropped off around the corner, paid cash and bugged out. The driver had the impression that the guy was frantic for his sister's safety because as soon as he paid, he ran off in the direction of the courthouse. The driver also called the police. We have a record of his 911 call coming in just after it all happened."

"What about surveillance tape from the pickup or drop-off sites?" Cormac's question was succinct.

"We haven't been able to locate any. Officers are still canvassing."

The brothers exchanged a serious glance, and Emily

knew any hope she had that everyone would just blow off her little incident as a fluke—so that she could try to convince herself that was all it was—had died a painful death.

Until they found her would-be abductor, she was in real danger.

From him. And from her forced proximity to Cormac Colton, too.

The intensity of feelings the private investigator raised in her should have been criminal.

The two cases Sean was most interested in, as far as Emily's involvement was concerned, were the two he was also most familiar with—the one involving Humphrey Kelly's testimony and the Lana Brinkley murder that Sean had had to turn over to investigate the Kelly disappearance.

The case involving Kelly's testimony had been put on hold due to the psychiatrist's absence, just until another expert could be called in to take Kelly's place, but taking Emily out of the picture wouldn't make any difference to that or in any way prevent the district from continuing on with the trial. With her gone, another ADA would simply be assigned to take over for her.

Same with the Brinkley murder, in terms of trial, but if Emily was on to something there that their prime suspect, Wall Street mogul Wes Westmore, didn't want getting out, he could have hired someone to get to Emily. To intimidate her into silencing some evidence he might suspect she had. Westmore had just recently been arrested and was now in prison awaiting trial.

"I can't imagine what it would be," Emily told Sean as Cormac reached to the file cabinet in the closet behind his table, spun the dial to unlock it and pulled out his Westmore file.

He liked things spread out in front of him, where he could take them in all at once, a big picture, rather than flipping back and forth between screens.

"You all have more on the case than I do," she said, opening her own Westmore file. "But I'm still going through it all, so there might be something here I'm going to pick up on. I'll jump in again as soon as we're done here."

A fist tightening in Cormac's gut had him biting his tongue rather than suggest that Emily take a day or two off from work. At least until he'd had time to get a handle on things—both the kidnapping attempt and the baby she was carrying.

She wouldn't listen to him.

And truth was, he wasn't sure she should. As long as she worked from his place, she'd be reasonably safe. He didn't have a say in the rest of her choices.

Except…she did plan to have the baby, didn't she?

Did she even know?

He hoped she'd let him have a say in that.

And in what would happen to the child after it was born.

If she didn't want it, he'd take it.

And if she did…he'd insist on doing his part.

Thoughts flew as Emily let Sean know that she wasn't thrilled that he was off the Brinkley case. And with a blink, Cormac wondered how he could know, in the space of an hour or two, that he was ready to commit himself to being a father.

Well, not ready, at all, but committed to getting that way. He'd lost his dad young. Knew what it was like to get through high school without one. He wasn't doing that to his own kid.

"No offense, but I think Mitch Mallard is a blowhard," Emily was telling Sean, talking to Cormac's older brother as though they were familiar associates.

He supposed they could be. Just…when she and Cormac had been together, she'd never mentioned his brother.

But then, neither had he. Quite purposely.

Family didn't play into what they had going on.

Family was the antithesis of it.

And they'd made a kid from that?

He'd long ago lost any fondness he'd had for fate. But this…twist of circumstance…well it…blew.

But… "We share your opinion of Mitch." Cormac jumped back into the conversation—to put an abrupt end to his own internal wanderings, but also to tell her what his brother technically could not.

"With the attempted kidnapping happening so close to the courthouse, we have to consider that the perp could be someone within the courthouse," he said then, something that had occurred to him on the ride home. "Someone who knows your schedule." He spoke to his new houseguest but looked to his brother as well.

Sean nodded before asking, "Can you think of anyone there that might have it in for you for some reason? Not necessarily work related."

The way Emily's brow furrowed when she was looking for answers had been one of the initial things that had attracted his attention the first time he'd worked with her. The shape of her brows accented those big dark eyes, until they were pools he could drown in.

And he nearly had, the first time he'd jumped in. He'd come close to throwing away everything that mattered most to him, to forgetting all the painful lessons he'd learned. Had barely been able to get himself out.

No way he could go back in…

"Not that I can… I mean, there's this guy in the DA's office. He's young, egotistical, a good mind, but needs to slow down and think before he speaks if he hopes to make it… Anyway, he made a big deal about discovering some evidence that turned a case into something else entirely, one of my cases, and tried to go over my head to get his day in the sun, but it turned out that he almost blew my case and I called him on it. In front of people."

"What's this guy's name?" Cormac asked.

"Jason Willoughby."

"I'll look into him," Cormac told them.

"You think it could be him? That this was just payback for embarrassing him?"

"If it was, don't for one second think that it means you're in less danger," Sean interjected. "Someone who'd go to those lengths to get back at a colleague…there's no telling what else he might do."

The stark expression that flitted across Emily's face made Cormac want to shut his brother up, even though he knew he'd have given her the same warning if Sean hadn't spoken first.

"The incident did have a personal feel about it," he said then.

"He wasn't just dragging me into the car, he was holding me up against him," Emily added slowly, looking between the two of them. "I didn't even think about that until now."

Sean nodded, then offered, "Could be the only way he could get you into the car."

"Yeah, but the way he told her he'd get her next time…

I heard his words," Cormac spoke up. "It sounded like he had it in for her. Like he was making a promise specifically to her, not just to an ADA on a case. I heard real intensity in his voice. We'll make a list of all possibilities from cases, but I want to pursue this personal angle, too," he told his brother.

Sean nodded, as Cormac had known he would. His brother might have age and experience on him, but he knew that Sean also respected his judgment implicitly. That the detective respected and relied on him.

As did a whole lot of other people.

Which was precisely why he would never again lose his mind to the vagaries of being in love, or even getting caught up in a long-term one-on-one partnership.

The reminder couldn't have come at a better time.

Standing, Sean nodded at Cormac and then, to Emily, said, "Keep me posted on whatever you come up with on the Westmore case," he said. "And if you think of anything…no matter how small…on the Kelly case…"

Emily nodded. "I will." Her tone was different when she spoke to Sean. More distant.

Somehow Cormac had to get her to talk to him like that, too.

"And listen to this guy," Sean said then, punching Cormac lightly on the shoulder. "He might be a pain in the ass, but he's the best there is at what he does. If anyone can find your answers and also get you through this unscathed, it's him."

It had been a while since Cormac had had the urge to deck his big brother. But that urge came knocking, hard, as he stood and, avoiding even a glance at Emily, practically pushed Sean toward the door.

He was no kid to be teased by his big brother—huge compliment included or not.

He might be eleven years younger than his recent lover, but when it came to the situations they were now facing, both the risk to her life and the kid she was carrying, they were complete equals.

Chapter 5

She went through her cases, reread notes she'd made to herself and flagged the ones that had anything that seemed the least acrimonious to her before passing them on to Cormac. And then she looked at the list Cormac gave her that he'd compiled of recent prison releases from cases that had her name listed, either as ADA, or even back in her earlier days when she was second chair.

She pulled out a couple of names from his list. "This Blake Nygren. He was one of those guys that stared at you the whole time. Trying to intimidate you with his threatening looks every minute you were in court prosecuting him."

Shaking her head, she circled the name and moved on. Couldn't sit there with the memories the name brought back. The nights she'd lain in bed fearing for her life, imagining who on his crew he'd call to stop her from putting away their boss.

"And Julius Hemming. He referred to me by his version of my first name, Bitch, more than once. And told me that I'd pay for what I was doing to him. He insisted that he was innocent."

"Is there a chance he was?"

Shaking her head, she shrugged, too. And said, "Without a confession or video, there's always a chance, isn't there? That something wrong happened with forensics on a case? Or someone lied about what they saw. Maybe ballistics weren't right." She said it because she was talking to Cormac. The man had a way of loosening her tongue like no one else had. Ever.

She'd felt safe talking to him. As though he wouldn't use her words against her. Read things into them that weren't there. Or judge her by them, either.

Not that she'd thought everyone else in her life did. Until Cormac's advent into her world, she hadn't even known she'd watched everything she said around everyone.

Until, with him, she hadn't.

They'd talked about everything.

Because there'd been nothing attached to any of it. They were two rocks on the same beach, until the tide came in and swept them eternally apart.

The tide. Not Cormac. The fact that their liaison had come to an end was not the issue. They'd known going in that it would happen. Had both only gone in because they could *count* on the fact that it would happen. But in the future.

Not abruptly. Cold turkey. After only a week.

Corman, not the tide, had told her it was best if they didn't stay in touch, or even speak again.

Sean had been gone a couple of hours and Cormac

hadn't said a word to her that wasn't case related. He'd told her, after a call from Sean, that Jason Willoughby, the young attorney who'd tried to upstage her, had left the DA's office a few months before and moved out of state. But he said little else, as they'd both been focused on getting through her information, looking for suspects.

"I'm not going to take your money," Cormac's words came out of the blue. "Me protecting you, it's personal. The right thing to do. I'm protecting my kid, too."

"And how are you going to explain that to anyone else?"

He nodded. "I know. I get why you said what you did. But between you and me, I'm not taking your money."

She wanted to argue the point. But decided it wasn't worth the battle when there were so many in front of them. If she chose to pay him, she would. What he did with the money was up to him.

She turned back to her list.

"Look over the names carefully," he said, coming around to her side of the table, to look at the document on her screen—the list he'd just emailed her, complete with case number references and key data attached for each possible suspect.

She was already working her way farther down the list but started to share her thoughts aloud.

"James Kinney. That's a no. He's seventy, had a nasty temper when he drank, but was a model prisoner and has been dry for five years. I spoke in his favor at his parole hearing. Myles Garcia, maybe, but I don't see it. He's a drug dealer, not a killer. I could see him spitting on me, but he's too small-time to have any crew, and too short to have done this himself. Peter Bezos, no. He's white collar, a now disbarred lawyer, who had some wrong clients. It was a slippery slope thing and I recommended the lightest sentence in a place where he'd be safe. He sent me a letter from prison thanking me for my treatment of him."

Cormac's deodorant, or soap or something, was slowly infiltrating her system. With every breath she took, more of him became more of her. To the point that, for a second there, they were transported back a couple of months, working together and on the verge of becoming something she'd never thought she could be.

"Eugene Maxwell," she blurted, a bit roughly, "is a possibility. He shot the guy who killed his cousin, claiming that if I'd done my job right, the dead man would be the one going to jail. His attorney heard him tell his wife that one day I'd know what it felt like to be on the wrong side and not get a fair shake."

"You prosecuted the guy who killed his cousin, didn't win, and then he killed the guy?"

"Yeah. It was a turf-war drug deal gone bad. The claim was that the cousin wasn't part of it. Just in the wrong place at the wrong time and ended up with a bullet. But the case was all circumstantial, based on unreliable witness testimony. Anyone who was really there, who knew what had happened, wasn't talking."

"Who was the detective on it?"

"Mitch Mallard." As soon as she started to say the name, she glanced at Cormac and found him staring at her, too. The man they'd all agreed they weren't happy to have on the Brinkley case in Sean's stead. The man did his job well enough to stay employed, but even that was a stretch.

"The Brinkley case is as high profile as it gets," Emily said, holding Cormac's gaze as he took a step back, but stayed focused on her. "All over social media…"

"It's pretty much all everyone's talking about," he agreed.

"And Mallard has given me nothing more on it. Nothing. Everything I have is from Sean. The guy's, at best, lazy as hell. Dragging his feet on what could be the most notorious case of his career…"

"And if you follow through on that, you have to wonder, if he's a slacker on a high-profile case, how much effort would he put into prosecuting the killer of a guy suspected of drug connections with no one who seemed to care except a cousin…"

"Right." Cormac had stood upright, but was still there. Close enough that she could touch him if she reached out. Watching her.

While she watched him back.

And then, abruptly, he was around the table, grabbing his laptop. "I'm going back to my room to make some calls," he said. "I don't want to interrupt your concentration. Hopefully by the time we meet again, I'll have an alibi for Eugene Maxwell, or Sean will have an arrest warrant. In the meantime, take one more look at that list, just in case…"

An arrest warrant?

It could all be over just that quickly?

While relief spread through her, profound relief, leaving her somewhat weak in the knees, Emily wasn't completely overjoyed.

She was…a little disappointed.

Which made no sense at all.

Unless, some small part of her heart had wanted the excuse to be close to Cormac Colton while she got over the shock of finding out that she was having his baby.

Because she didn't have a lot of time for shock. More

to the point, she had to be working through the logistics of how a voraciously independent forty-three-year-old New York City ADA was going to continue to excel at her job while growing and having a baby, and then while raising the child alone.

She had no doubt she'd do it.

She just needed time to figure it all out.

"Eugene Maxwell has no alibi." Cormac hadn't had nearly the time away from Emily he'd needed, but the two hours he'd taken had helped some.

Focusing his mind on work had always been the cure. Mental concentration had been the only way the fourteen-year-old him had survived the death of his father, then later the wrong roads his twin had taken, followed by the death of a woman Cormac had firmly believed he'd be growing old with.

"He says he was at home alone and no one can verify that," he continued, glancing at the folders and notes scattered around the laptop currently open on his dining room table, rather than looking at the woman to whom they belonged.

Peripheral vision told him Emily was watching him. With pursed lips, he continued to move through the room, giving him an excuse not to meet her gaze directly. "He's been interviewed, they had to let him go."

"There wasn't enough cause to hold him," his unexpected houseguest concluded. As ADA, she'd know as well as anyone how it all worked.

It wouldn't make the circumstance any easier to swallow. He knew the only way she'd be able to feel safe, to go home, was to have the morning's evildoer behind bars.

And maybe to have Cormac gone for a bit. Lord knew, he needed some air to breathe that wasn't mingling with hers.

"I have to go out for a bit," he told her, raising his voice just enough to be heard as he continued through the room toward the door. "The department has assigned a detail to sit outside the building until this guy's caught, and while I'm gone, there will be someone patrolling this floor, too."

He'd already had her put him and Sean on speed dial.

He paused by the door. "I've got a meeting with my siblings on the Kelly case." He owed her no explanation.

Had specifically decided not to report in to her, except where it directly involved her. They weren't a team. A family.

Or even roommates.

They were…he didn't know what.

People who would barely speak to each other, having a baby, seemed to be the route she wanted to take. He'd tried to bring up the subject on the drive to his apartment, trying to grasp who he'd just become, to process the fact that his world had just changed dramatically. Drastically. Forever. Separate and apart from her.

He was going to be a father.

He had no idea where he'd fit into the plan.

And he needed to know.

She'd shut down the conversation in the car. And again, when he'd tried, after they'd entered his apartment…

He had to get out.

He reached for the door handle.

"Cormac." Her tone was a little louder, as his had just been. Filled with authority. Like a court voice.

"Yeah?" He spun around, was glad to see that, while she'd turned in her chair, she wasn't coming any closer to him.

"Please don't tell your siblings about the baby."

He'd had zero plans to…wasn't anywhere near even thinking about that yet. But he was not fool enough to walk away from an open door. "They're biologically related. They have a right to know." He had rights to conversation with her about it all.

A look of consternation, followed by vulnerability, crossed her face. He'd never seen either before, and his gut clenched. What an ass he was being. Thinking about his needs. His fatherhood. She had to be nearly as shocked as he was, since she'd expected negative test results, and her immediate role in their monumental development was far more encompassing than his.

"But… I didn't intend to tell anyone about it. For now."

Her nod, the flash of relief—of…gratitude?—she sent his way had him throwing up his own defenses again. Against the intensity of the emotions she raised in him all across the board.

What in the hell made her so different? And how did he diffuse her power over him?

"But we need to talk," he said then, taking a stance for his own sense of control. "Soon."

"I've got the case of my career sitting before me, and a maniac out to get me, Cormac. The rest…there's time later for any conversation we might need to have."

What in the hell did that mean? Might need to?

"You…you're thinking about not having the baby?" He tensed, waiting.

"No. I'm not considering that option." Just that. Nothing else. She turned back to her computer and started typing.

She was... Emotions swirled faster than thought. How did he move forward, know what steps to take, what thoughts to dwell on, while being so critically cut out of his major life event?

Knowing her, he understood her reticence. In any other case he would have welcomed it. They were alike that way. Did he come across as inaccessible to others as she was seeming to him right then?

How could she just turn her back on what seemed to him to be his moral right to be involved in, something that was so intimately personal to him?

Hating his sense of helplessness, feeling more like a wounded animal than his usual impenetrable self, he left without another word.

Emily's shoulders slumped as soon as she heard the click of the door lock behind Cormac. Finally, for the first time since she'd seen the test results, she had a few minutes wholly to herself.

Not as welcome as they'd have been in her own home, but at least she was alone...

At first, she relaxed. Welcomed the respite from being under Colton's scrutiny—even from another room, Cormac's ability to see and know and figure out was intimidating.

Then she started to shake. Which wasn't acceptable.

Jumping up, she explored the kitchen she'd had in view from her seat at the table. Looked through the cupboards she knew Cormac used for dry goods, then took stock of the contents in the refrigerator and freezer, too.

She was shocked to find the two thick salmon filets

she'd bagged up and left in his freezer after dinner one night, thinking, at the time, that they'd have them together the next time she was over.

There she was, her next night over, and there the salmon was, too. Blinking away tears, she shut the freezer, not at all amused by this one of life's little ironies.

The night she'd made that salmon she'd been standing in that very kitchen, thinking about how incredible life was, to give her exactly what she needed. A man she didn't have to worry about hurting. One who would never, ever open his heart up to her so completely that she had the possibility of breaking it. One who'd never need more from her than the leftovers.

Because her job always got first dibs.

For that week with him, she'd been so happy. More so than she could ever remember being. Even as a child with her idyllic upbringing.

And now…she had a child? Just growing inside her, yeah, but…there. Already needing things from her.

A human being who would have to come first.

Who would pull her away from her life's work. Her life's purpose.

That alone was more than she could contemplate.

And Cormac wanted to talk? To figure out…what? The kind of mother she could be?

How could she possibly talk about something she knew nothing about? Or give him what she didn't have?

Answers.

She couldn't even be a successful partner in an adult relationship—as was proven by the severely damaged heart she'd left behind when she'd been Cormac's age, the young vibrant college professor she'd promised to marry who'd ended up with a heart jaded by her inability to put personal life before work—how could she possibly be responsible for raising a helpless innocent?

One step at a time, she left the kitchen. She sat back down to work at the dining room table.

One step at a time was how she found the truth lurking inside of every case she'd ever had.

So...one step at a time.

And the first step wasn't knowing all the answers. It was calling her doctor and making an appointment to get in to see her as soon as possible.

She couldn't begin to make plans without all the facts.

And if Cormac wanted more, he was going to have to wait. She'd already given him the one truth she had, when they were together before and creating the current situation. With what she gave to her job, she didn't have much left to give to relationships in her life. She would be stretched even thinner with a baby needing her.

She wasn't going to make promises, even small ones, that she couldn't keep.

Chapter 6

The diner was busy. It could have been one of a number of New York City diners the siblings had been to before. The location chosen by Sean based on an appointment he had to keep.

Cormac, who generally didn't bother himself with answers that were none of his business, didn't need to know more than that.

What he needed most desperately to know, the ADA wasn't sharing.

He was the last to arrive and shrugged out of his overcoat as he approached the square table in the back corner of the brightly lit, crowded room. Throwing the coat over the same rack that held ones he recognized as his siblings', he ordered hot chocolate and sat.

Eva, in uniform on his left, was saying something to Liam on her other side, giving Cormac the chance to lean over to Sean on his right and ask if Eugene Maxwell had made any moves, calls or visits since he'd left the interview room.

"Not that I've heard, but the guy's wife left him while he was in prison and is married to someone else in the neighborhood, which has got to be stirring up bad emotions every minute he's home, so I'm liking him for our guy," Sean answered. As he and Cormac glanced at the table and saw their two siblings watching them, Sean filled the other two in on the details of Emily's case as well.

They all knew her. As the ADA.

None of them knew Cormac had slept with the woman for one glorious week. Or even that they'd ever had a friendly meal together.

His time with Emily…it hadn't been for sharing, most particularly not with family. It hadn't been going anywhere that would involve family. Ever.

Just imagining the ribbing he'd have taken, him doing a woman eleven years older than him…

Except that…a *baby*?

They were going to be aunt and uncles…

Shivering from a boatload of trussed up emotion, blowing it off as a chill coming in with him from outside, he opened his menu, wondering how he was going to explain having no appetite at all.

But he didn't have to worry about that small problem as Sean started talking and all four of the siblings chose not to order meals. Cormac knew the others well enough to know that the subject of Humphrey's continued absence stripped all of them of any desire for food.

Sean, still in the tan pants and white shirt he'd had on earlier at Cormac's place, started right in. "I know we all have places to be, so I'm going to be brief. We still haven't had a single sighting of Humphrey reported, not even on the tip line, and there's been no word from a kidnapper, no ransom demand."

"I hate to say it, but it's time to start preparing ourselves for the worst," Liam added. "Humphrey wouldn't have just left of his own accord, no way he's walking out on us, let alone his new young wife, and his patients. And with no ransom demand, it means he's probably already been...dealt with. Depending on who got to him, we might never find the body."

Trying to kick his twin under the table, Cormac felt Eva's tension even before their little sister's eyes filled with tears. When the table fell instantly silent, with all three brothers assessing the damage, Eva jumped up and made a beeline for the bathroom.

"Way to go, bro," Cormac said with a downward smirk of his mouth. Yeah, Eva was a cop now, but at six years his and Liam's junior, she'd always be their baby sister first. "The kid was eight when Dad died. Humphrey is pretty much the only parent she knows..."

"He's right," Sean butted in between them before Liam could get hot. Or not. With his green gaze claiming them both, Sean put on his stern face, the short-haired look he was going with these days adding to his air of authority over them. "Or rather, you're both right. Liam's right first. We do need to be prepared. And we're all going to have to look after Eva..."

Cormac would have given his older brother a lighter, warning kick if he'd had a chance.

"No one has to look out for me," Eva said as she calmly reclaimed her seat, her pinned back long red hair giving her an air of composure. "If I'm going to make it as an

NYPD cop, and I *am* going to make it, I'm going to have to get tougher."

Cormac got it. All of it. Her need to be a cop. Her need for toughness. "But not too tough, okay?" he asked hesitantly, with a tad of softness in the tone reserved only for her.

Before she could respond, Sean took over again with, "Like he's one to talk. No one's more jaded than Cormac."

With a shrug and a grimace, Cormac took the assessment on the chin, knowing that his brother was right. He let the emotional moment die, as Sean had meant it to do.

He could have defended himself with justifications, but his siblings already knew about the very personal betrayal that had hit him the hardest. And with the violence on the streets, he spent his days in way more of the daily grit than Sean or Liam did. A lot of what he dealt with never even made it to a detective's desk. Yeah, that made a guy jaded.

Not at all daddy material…

The thought crept through, but Cormac was able to push it aside almost instantly as Liam told them, "I managed to get a list of every one of Humphrey's clients," and then added, "Don't ask me how," before anyone, mostly Eva, who was a huge stickler for protocol, could question him. Leaning in, Liam turned his potent blue-eyed gaze on each of them individually, one at a time, and said, "The list is more dangerous than we ever suspected. There are Wall Street sharks who've done prison time for fraud and insider trading. On top of that he had more than a few clients who are criminally insane, and there are some real doozies in between, too." Pulling pages from his notebook, he handed them each one. "I figured we'd split up the list."

"Good idea," Sean said, his expression clearly concerned as he glanced over his list. "Let's investigate everyone on our lists, looking for possible motives, for any way they'd benefit by Humphrey being permanently gone."

"Or benefit from holding Humphrey captive for a length of time," Cormac added, the fact that his little sister was sitting next to him, driving him to remind them all of that other very real possibility.

"I think that's what we're all hanging on to at the moment," Sean agreed. The four of them exchanged glances, and just like that, they were as one.

As they'd always been and always would be.

The only family unit Cormac had ever expected, or wanted, to have.

With her doctor appointment on the books, Emily did what she always did. She worked. Specifically, going over evidence in the Brinkley murder.

And by the time she heard Cormac's key in the lock, she'd already made a call to set up an appointment within the next forty-eight hours with a witness who'd recanted a statement she'd given at the beginning of the investigation. Just that one statement could break the case wide-open. In the truth's—and the state's—favor.

In the middle of a nervous conversation with herself regarding whether or not to tell Cormac she was arranging the meeting, at least until it was actually on the calendar, she was interrupted by the ringing of her phone.

A receptionist from work. Someone who did occasional casework for Emily.

"Yeah, Sarah, what's up?" She took the call as Cormac closed the door, shutting them alone together in his apartment.

Sarah knew she was always welcome to call. But she only did so when it was important.

"I'm sorry to bother you…" she heard the usual fatigue in the much younger woman's words, and instead of feeling the usual compassion, horror plummeted Emily's stomach contents. Twins. Sarah was the single mother of four-year-old twins. A woman who loved her job, who was good at it, but whose exhaustion showed more days than not.

Cormac was a twin.

Were there two babies growing inside Emily? Fathoming just one was…

"It's just that, you didn't come back today, and these roses were left for you. I just thought you'd want to know…"

"Roses?" What roses?

Cormac, who'd seemed to be passing through to the kitchen, stopped and looked at her.

Giving him a shrug, Emily put the phone on speaker.

"They're really pretty, and expensive looking, and if they don't get in some water, they're going to die. I can take them home with me if you'd like…"

With a raised eyebrow, Cormac continued to stand there, making her uncomfortable for totally unprofessional reasons. Whether he thought so or not, she was not in the habit of getting roses at work.

The occasion was another first in a day filled with bad ones.

"Who are they from?" she asked, expecting to hear that a family to whom she'd brought justice had just happened to choose that day to express over and above gratitude. Even when fate was raining on you, it could bring sunshine, too.

One baby, please, instead of two?

"I…um, thought you'd know…" Sarah's tone sounded uncomfortable. "I couldn't help but read the card, it was just there…"

With a completely different kind of knot filling her stomach, made worse by the sharpening of Cormac's gaze, Emily responded with, "Read it to me."

"Okay, but…it says, 'Sweet scent for my sweet. Beauty for a beauty. I loved the feel of your body against mine, dearest Emily. I'll be counting the hours until next time.'"

Her gaze locked with Cormac's as her trembling fingers forced her to set the phone down. "Who's it from?" He barked the question.

"Excuse me? Who's this?" There was no weariness evident in Sarah's sharpened tone.

"It's Cormac Colton, Sarah. After the situation outside the courthouse today, I've hired him for protection."

"I heard about the attempted abduction, Emily, and I've been thinking about you all day. When you didn't come back, I was worried…"

"I'm fine. Just working remotely while the police try to pin down the whys of what happened. Out of an abundance of caution," she added the overused phrase.

"Who signed the card?" Colton asked again, kindlier.

"No one." Sarah's words carried new worry. "You don't… I thought it was a date…"

She hadn't had a date in months. Two of them to be exact.

And the one prior to Cormac Colton had been that many years in the past. At least.

It was a testimony to her state of mind that she admitted as much aloud. With enough wherewithal to leave out

Cormac's identity when she referred to the short liaison they'd shared as one outing.

Looking back, it had seemed that way. A dinner that had turned into spending together every waking moment that neither of them were working. With as much as both of them worked, they'd either had to spend their off hours together or not see each other.

She was seeing plenty of him right then. He wore a tight-lipped expression as he tempered a tone she could see rising to a yell as he asked, "Did you see who delivered the flowers?"

"Yes, of course. I was right here," Sarah answered him. "A woman, in her thirties. Said she was here to get a marriage license. She told me that a guy handed them to her outside, and he said that if Emily saw him, it would ruin the surprise. Plus, he didn't want to embarrass her at work."

"Did she say what he looked like?" Cormac was standing over the phone.

"No, but I didn't ask. I just thought..." Sarah's voice trailed off, leaving all three of them to know what she'd thought.

"What time was this?" Cormac's next question kicked Emily into gear, too. They could access the surveillance camera outside the building.

"Around one," Sarah replied without hesitation. "I was just getting back from lunch."

"Good, can you do me a favor?" While Emily was still trying to catch up to her professional self, reeling from the note on the card and the obvious conclusion, Cormac's questions just kept coming.

"I'll do whatever I can." Sarah was right there, ready

to do his bidding. As were any of the other women she'd ever seen the man having dealings with.

"Can you check and see who applied for a marriage license today at one?"

"I'd need a warrant to pass on that information."

"I'll have one to you within the half hour."

Without another word, Cormac turned from the table, leaving the dining room as he dialed his phone.

And for the first time that day Emily was one hundred percent glad that he was sharing her space.

The fiend had been taunting her with those flowers. Spinning his foiled abduction, his body pressed against hers, as a win for him, something that gave him pleasure. A step forward rather than a step back. He'd made it personal, and as violating as possible. Instead of losing confidence due to failure, the man had rallied and attacked from afar, just a couple of hours later.

And had been bold enough to show himself with a bouquet of flowers in front of her office building.

Cormac made his calls, tracking down one source while he waited for callbacks from others, but as soon as he'd received his answers, he got right back out to the living room, needing to keep Emily in his sight.

With the patrol outside, he knew she was safe. The knowledge didn't stop the drive to protect her that was pulsing through him at such a pace he couldn't sit still. She was not only a woman he admired greatly, she was going to be the mother of his child.

A fact he couldn't process any more than the idea that if he hadn't happened to be heading to her office at the exact time he had that morning, she could already be dead.

Or at least missing.

The vagaries of fate, of life, didn't sit well with him.

Nor did the way Emily Hernandez was shutting him out. She hadn't even glanced up from her computer when he'd walked back into the room.

"Sean got warrants," he said, plopping his butt in the chair at the end of the dining table, perpendicular to her. Facing the side of her cheek.

Staring because he couldn't just walk away and leave her alone. As much as she seemed to want that. He couldn't pretend that the baby didn't exist. Or that they didn't have a mutual critical life change happening between them. There were things to discuss. The baby wasn't just hers.

And while he wouldn't be physically housing the kid, he still had to do all he could to assist her in doing so. Whatever that meant.

Grocery shopping maybe. Providing healthy meals. There had to be takeout for pregnant women. He could arrange daily...

She turned her head. Was finally looking at him.

And he realized he'd mentioned the warrants and nothing else.

"The guy stayed out of view of surveillance cameras positioned outside your office."

"How could that be? There are enough of them to take in pretty much the whole area."

He'd had a similar response when he'd first heard the news. "There are a couple of missed areas. But you'd have to know exactly where they are to avoid being seen. Which leads us to believe this guy is someone who frequents the DA's office on a regular basis. For all we know, he might not be someone case related, but rather, someone you see every day. Maybe even someone you work with."

His gut didn't buy it. Still, the possibility was there, so it had to be managed.

The brown in Emily's eyes intensified when she was flooding with emotion. Passion, or fear apparently. "I can't think of anyone who's shown any interest," she told him.

"No one's asked you out? Or maybe even offered to do a favor or something at work that you've turned down?"

Shaking her head slowly, she glanced at her computer and then back, her suited shoulders suddenly seeming fragile to him covered in the long dark waves that had wisped along his body on more than one occasion. "Seriously, I'm always so swamped that anytime anyone offers any help, I gladly accept."

"And dinner invitations? Do you get them, too?"

The question was necessary. His tension as he awaited her response had nothing at all to do with the case.

"Not in years," she said. "I meant it when I told you that I don't date anyone involved in any way with my work."

She *had* told him that. The first time he'd asked her to have a drink with him. But her gaze, it had already been smoldering, and he'd been certain that the fire pulsing through him had been lit by one alight in her.

He hadn't asked a second time.

She had. The day he'd finished his investigation into a woman set to testify for her. She'd called half an hour after he'd turned in his final report.

"I can see where that might be hard for you to believe." The words came out now with a thickness not normally present. As though her throat was dry. "That I don't date anyone related to my work."

And her gaze was pinned on him again. Almost as though she was finding it as impossible as he was to stay away.

As though the two months they'd put between them hadn't quashed even a tiny bit of the weird bond they'd shared.

He'd smothered the inferno and it was still raging?

"I swear to you, I've made my position clear for so long, no one ever even asks me to have a drink in a group after a case."

Now, that just sounded…lonely.

"But you go out for drinks…" He'd seen her once, in a bar by the courthouse, a couple of weeks after he'd ditched her. And had turned around and left before she saw him.

He'd come back to his apartment and gotten drunk.

It hadn't helped.

"With the same group of girlfriends, yes. Other attorneys, mostly."

"Have you told any of them about the pregnancy?" The question wasn't planned, just spilled out naturally, broaching the subject he most needed to discuss with her.

As long as her life was in danger, his baby's was, too, and she had to understand that. Not go on thinking that he was some kind of freak out to control her, or cage her, or in any way impinge on her independence.

"Of course not. There'd be questions and since I don't even have answers for myself, I can hardly be prepared to stave off others'."

He got that. Really got it. Nodded.

"Another theory…from…uh…the flowers…is that the guy knew nothing about camera placement, but got lucky enough to be behind someone taller than him, or was hidden from view by a large group of what looked like law students entering the building."

"And there are the couple of pillars that block views," she said quickly, with a little too much force. Like her words were tumbling over themselves to get past the ones they weren't letting out.

"We did get a description of him from the woman who delivered the flowers." Leaning in, resting his forearms on the table, Cormac folded his hands. "It was pretty much what we had from this morning. Average height, maybe six feet, winter coat—but it wasn't leather. Hood and scarf, like this morning. She said the scarf was brown, not black."

"Witnesses confuse things like that all the time." She stated the obvious, her tone…nervous. Fidgeting. Just like the fingers that were rubbing back and forth along the edge of her laptop. "But all of this…it fits Eugene Maxwell."

Exactly.

"Having been at the DA's office frequently when he'd been testifying in the trial for his cousin's killer he'd be familiar with the building's security. When he'd been charged with murder himself, there was earlier surveillance camera footage on the news, showing him heading into the building," she said. "I'd been coming up the steps of our building with morning coffee, and he'd been coming in for deposition. He approached me. His attorney later tried to say that his own trial was tainted, to get me off the case, because of that outside encounter, but after he'd viewed the tape he'd seen that the surveillance footage not only didn't show him, it showed that I never even looked at anyone, let alone talked to them."

While Cormac might have found it hard to believe

that anyone could hear someone call out to them and not glance over, he could believe it of Emily. When she was focused on a case, it was like nothing else existed.

He'd seen her switch from lover to prosecutor with the ring of a phone.

Had admired the hell out of her for it.

Because it meant that she was like him.

It meant that he didn't ever have to worry about "them" becoming more than burning hot sex with some admiration and friendliness thrown in.

And he hadn't known that about the surveillance tape. Hadn't known that Maxwell would have been privy to the placement of cameras when he'd figured him for delivering the flowers.

What resonated for him was Maxwell's divorce. "The man lost his wife because of his own guilty verdict," he said. "Now, not only does he not get any loving of his own, after having been locked up with men for years, but he also has to live down the street from his ex-wife living with another man."

"It makes sense that he'd make sexually charged threats against the woman he holds responsible for ruining his marriage," she finished. "What do you think?"

He thought that he had to find something to prove that Maxwell needed to be back in prison before the man had another chance to get close to Emily.

"I think we need to talk about you being pregnant with my kid."

Chapter 7

"What about the florist? Is someone checking florists in the area? Long-stemmed red roses almost two weeks before Valentine's Day, someone might remember him. He could have paid with a credit card."

Not baby talk. She wasn't ready.

She hadn't assimilated enough rational or clear thoughts to have the conversation with herself yet, let alone anyone else.

"They weren't florist quality, they were in cellophane with a rubber band holding them together. Typical bodega bouquet, or maybe from a subway stop. We can hope subway stop. There'll be surveillance cameras and there are fewer subway florists than bodegas. In any case, Sean has officers canvasing…"

"Maxwell wouldn't have been able to afford anything but a cheap bouquet," she said, half to herself. It all made sense. And she was relieved to know that they still had a viable lead, no matter how small. It gave her hope. "They're checking his neighborhood bodegas, right?"

"Yeah, and between there and the courthouse, too."

Good. For a second there, she felt almost normal. An ADA sitting at her computer, enmeshed in her case files, getting filled in by a professional on an ongoing investigation.

"We have to talk about it, Emily."

He hadn't moved. Neither had she. But they were no longer at the office. Even a home one.

"No, we don't."

"That's not logical. You're an intelligent, savvy woman. You know this isn't going to go away. You can't just take your luck and disappear. The kid's mine, too. The responsibility is mine."

She couldn't listen to him. Not yet. "The body's mine." And it was a hell of a lot older than his.

His sigh wasn't encouraging. It sounded like frustration, not compliance. He was a Colton. He wasn't giving up.

More to the point, he was Cormac. A person as determined as she was to be in control of his life, of his heart, at all times.

They couldn't both be in total control on this one.

At the moment, her position seemed more solid for being the one who could claim boss-hood.

"I'm only asking for conversation," he said, his tone rightly conciliatory.

She looked at him, met his gaze, and knew instantly she'd made a grave mistake. Her heart lurching in a way it never had before Cormac, she said, "You want to tell me exactly what to say to you? Because at the moment, I can probably repeat back to you what I've heard said, but other than that, you're asking for something I don't have."

"I just need to know what you're thinking."

"You and me, both." Exhausted, she met his gaze, letting him see whatever was in her eyes. "I'm not trying to be a pain in the ass. But you want answers and I don't have any. My system is still in the struggling for acceptance stage."

He held her gaze, and she held on to his, too. In those seconds, it was like their eyes were satisfying them with answers neither one of them had to give.

"Can we at least confirm that we're going to have it?"

Too much. Way too much. So many things could affect that outcome. She wasn't ready to think about any of them. But…his intense dark eyes pulled words up out of her. "We can confirm that I have no intention of purposefully terminating the pregnancy."

It was all she had.

Oh, and "And I hope we can confirm that no one but the two of us needs to know about this situation right now. At least not until we've had time to adjust to the news ourselves, to be better equipped to answer questions."

Like, what was a forty-three-year-old woman doing in bed with a thirty-two-year-old man? Well, not what, that was obvious. But…why?

One look at Cormac made that a little obvious, too. So maybe, the questions would be more in line with, why was a thirty-two-year-old man doing it with a forty-three-year-old woman?

"What about your parents?" He knew she had them. That they were happily retired in Florida. That she saw them once or twice a year but talked to them regularly.

And that she'd been an only child and had a great child-hood. Nothing more. Not even that her dad was a retired cop. Just the generics.

She shook her head. "Not until I know more."

His nod wasn't enough. "And your family?" she prod-ded, even though he'd already agreed not to tell them.

"No." He raised his hand from the table, reached out like maybe he'd take hers, but his palm fell back to the wood again. Empty. "Not until we have more of an idea of what it all means."

What it all means.

A bizarre way of describing a pregnancy.

Yet purely Cormac. The words reached her in long empty places. The baby wasn't a case to solve or answers to find to lead her to the right conclusions. He or she… meant something.

"You want salmon for dinner?" She wasn't hungry, but, at her age, carrying a child, no way she was going to skip a meal.

"If you're cooking. I'm not all that fond of the stuff, but with the sauce you baked it in last time…"

Last time. As his words dropped off, his look told her where his mind had gone, leaving them together in the middle of a sensual memory they both needed to forget.

He should have said he'd already eaten. Or insisted on ordering takeout—his usual mode of providing meals at home.

Smelling the salmon cooking, sitting down to eat it with her…all just reeked of things he'd spent two months forcing himself to forget.

He'd been happier for it, too. Better able to focus on

work. More peaceful. A trifle bored, perhaps. Missing the excitement.

But definitely better.

He'd saved himself from the depth of emotion that blinded him and could get folks killed.

Luckily for him, Emily seemed clearly as determined as him to forget the wildness they'd shared that one week in the beginning of December, probably remembering even better than he did how off it had been, how detrimental to the overall success of their individual lives.

They ate salmon but talked about Wes Westmore, the twenty-four-year-old slickly charming hedge fund millionaire on Wall Street who was as arrogant as he was good-looking. The man was currently sitting in a jail, a definite flight risk, while awaiting the upcoming trial where Emily was going to prosecute him for the murder of his girlfriend, Lana, who'd been found dead in his apartment.

Nothing about the senseless murder was understandable, or in any way palatable. And when Emily yawned, Cormac immediately insisted that they should turn in. She practically made a run for the spare bedroom, shutting herself inside before he'd turned out the lights and double-checked the front door, taking a peek out the living room curtain to ensure that their police detail was on the job.

He went to his bedroom but left the door open and worked for a few more hours, checking occasionally to see the light still on under her door. He found no connection between Evan Smith, the defendant awaiting a new psychiatric evaluation, and any other part of Humphrey's or Emily's life. Nor was there any obvious connection between the three people Smith had killed. From what he could see, the murders had been a result of simply way too much alcohol and testosterone overload. Smith didn't appear to have known the three people he'd killed in the bar fight that night.

Sometime close to midnight, he noticed the sliver of light gone from beneath Emily's door and told himself to lie down and go to sleep. He turned out the light, slid beneath his covers, and spent a good part of the night tossing and turning, dozing and waking, with an awareness of Emily, her body holding his child safely within her. He needed to do something.

He needed to make it all aboveboard, not something that had to be hidden.

He was taking a cold shower before dawn and was dressed in his usual jeans and thermal pullover and sucking down his second cup of coffee when Emily appeared, also in her usual apparel.

"You don't need business attire, working from home," he said, in lieu of the good morning that would have been more impersonally appropriate. The close-fitting navy pants, off-white silky blouse and jacket had him wanting to undress her in the worst way.

He'd already taken that exact outfit off her once before. Unzipping the heeled leather boots with his teeth. To her extreme pleasure.

And his.

"In the first place, business attire is pretty much my whole wardrobe. And in the second, I've got an appointment for an in-person interview this morning."

Whoa, what now? "An appointment? In person?" He knew shaking his head wasn't the best move with her. It shook anyway.

"I'm not on vacation, Cormac. The Westmore case is

going to trial, and I have to be ready for it. If that slime-ball walks, it's on me, and there's no way I'm going to let that happen. He killed a woman and somehow thinks he's entitled to get away with it."

He understood the extreme distaste in her tone. Agreed with it. But... "There are any number of people who know you're the ADA on the case. They know the witnesses. And we don't know who's after you." If he had to put it more bluntly, he would.

"I know. Which...is why I'm hoping you'll go with me to the interview." She blinked, looked away as she made the statement. Working him on the fly, he translated.

She no more wanted him accompanying her to work than he wanted to fall in love and get married for happily ever after.

"Of course I'll go," he said, accepting her compromise. Didn't matter whether she wanted him around or not. What mattered was that he would be guarding her body—and the life inside it as well.

And he hadn't even had to fight her on it.

Could it be that Emily Hernandez was finally realizing that she needed him?

Only professionally, of course.

Which was all he was after.

You didn't come home last night. Trying to hide from me? I like that. Playing hard to get. I'm up for the chase. It'll make getting you that much more rewarding.

Trembling, Emily read the text message as Cormac sat in the cab beside her. It had come in on her business cell. With no phone number attached.

"What's up?" Cormac's brow was creased with concern as he glanced from her to her phone.

Not now. Not in the cab.

"Why does anything have to be up?" She smiled, shook her head.

But then handed him the phone.

He read. His thumb flew across her screen, followed by other screens popping faster than she could decipher them. Then, handing her the phone, he pulled out his own, seemingly repeating the process, pausing after several seconds to read the screen.

By the time they arrived at the luxury apartment building in Tribeca, his phone was back in his pocket, and she was feeling...protected from the anonymous text.

He reached for his wallet, but she slid forward and paid the cab driver, then waited for him to vacate the car before following him out.

It felt weird, having him there. It made her uncomfortable on many levels. But she was glad he'd come along. For the moment, she needed him.

His professional services.

The text message...it unnerved her almost as much as the original abduction attempt. More than the flowers had done.

So much so that as they walked from the curb to the door of the building, she wanted to take Cormac's hand. To hold him close and hide herself against him. Which was probably why she let him so easily guide her in front of him and then keep a hand at her back as she showed her identification to the doorman, after which Cormac's hips beneath his jacket lightly grazed her coat-covered butt as he hurried them inside.

The flat expression on his face, the focus as he guided

her to the elevator, helped tamp down the fire that soft touch had raised in her, leaving her embarrassed with herself.

She was flooding with want and he obviously hadn't even noticed the miniscule contact.

Which was as it should be.

As she wanted it to be.

Needed it to be.

Chapter 8

Jeans were better when they weren't stretch or flexible. Good old stiff denim dissuaded a man's organ from growing too big too fast, and from maintaining the position. And while Cormac's jacket kept him warm enough, and the short length allowed ease for his legs to run as fast as they might need to, it was not serving him well as he stood in the otherwise deserted elevator with Emily.

Don't look down. Don't look down. Don't look down.

His brain sent the subliminal command to Emily over and over as he stared at the floor numbers, hoping that she'd continue to do so as well.

She moved, as though she might look down, and his hands dropped to a casual clasp in front of him.

Turned out her attention wasn't anywhere near his crotch. She'd moved her head, but to study the burlap lining the wall of the small space—the one closest to her and away from him.

Unless she had eyes in the back of her head, she wasn't seeing his hard-on.

And he shrank. A woman's lack of attention or appreciation tended to do that to a guy.

He'd never been more thankful to not be a magnet.

Or so he told himself as the door opened and they exited to a long, quiet, chandelier-lit, thickly carpeted hallway with only four doors, widely spaced apart.

His place was nice, overly spacious for the city, but this…

It was good if Emily wasn't attracted to him anymore. Very good. The best.

Maybe he'd imagined the heat between them the night before as they'd shared the rest of that salmon. Left over from the most memorably sensuous night of his life.

And what could he expect, really?

A woman with her experience…

Wait. Had he been a boy toy?

At the time, the thought had never occurred to him, but now…the way she kept blowing him off, refusing to talk like equals about the whole baby thing…

If she thought…

She'd already stopped in front of a door and rung the bell.

"Josie?" She asked as a woman peered through little more than the crack she'd opened in the doorway. Emily held up her card. "I'm Emily Hernandez," she said. And then, with a brief hesitation, glanced back at Cormac.

"Oh, and sorry, this is my…associate. I'm sorry I didn't tell you about him when we agreed to meet. I didn't realize he'd be accompanying me."

The door didn't open any wider. Emily had told him as they'd left his apartment that morning that Josie Deveraux was providing one of her strongest witness statements and had agreed readily to meet with her. The sooner the better.

That had been why Emily had been rushing out into the city just twenty-four hours after nearly being abducted, and before they had any sure leads on who'd tried to take her.

This Josie didn't seem at all ready to talk to anyone. To the contrary, he'd bet his gun that the woman wanted them gone. Immediately.

"Can we come in?" Emily asked, in her sweetest, most comforting-to-a-friendly-witness voice. He knew because she'd tried out all her voices on him one night as she sat on top of him while he filled her to the hilt.

And for each voice, there'd been a different movement...

What the hell...

Not the time.

"No. I...uh...have nothing to say to you." The woman's tone was strong. Almost angry. She moved to close the door.

And she probably would have if the toe of Emily's boot didn't slide forward, preventing the final click. "I really need to speak with you, Josie," she said then. "You said you liked Lana, that she was sweet. And your testimony is important to the case. We need to keep this guy out of this building, and off the streets, to make sure another Lana, maybe another friend of yours, doesn't fall for his line and end up just like Lana."

She was good.

But then, he knew that.

Josie opened the door only enough to stick her head out, appearing to take in the entire hallway.

Looking to see if anyone else was there?

"I can't talk to you right now," she said, not looking directly at either of them.

"So when would be a good time for me to come back?" Emily pressed.

"Never. I have nothing to say to you."

Senses alerting with each second that passed, Cormac focused on every nuance. He didn't like the repetition of phrase. It was as though the pretty young woman had been coached.

"You already gave your statement to the police." Emily's tone remained calm, soothing. Kind. "All I'm asking is for you to corroborate it for me so that I ask questions you can truthfully and easily answer while saying as little as possible. I want to make this as easy and quick for you as possible."

When Josie shook her head at that, Cormac knew what came next was not going to be good.

"The police misunderstood." Josie's hand on the doorknob pushed, but not as quickly as Emily's boot. The door remained wide enough to see the woman's full face. He looked for fear. Saw none.

But he didn't see much of anything else, either. A society woman trained to keep her emotions out of her expression?

Or someone simply telling the truth?

"You told the police you saw Wes Westmore hit Lana. How could they misunderstand that?"

"I don't know. They just did."

"You said they were on their way to the elevator, that one." Emily pointed from the direction they'd come. "Right here in this building. He hit her on the way. You saw it."

"I didn't see it." The woman stopped. Pressed her lips together, and then said, "I didn't see anything. I have no idea why they say I did."

"They also said you heard him threaten to kill Lana," Emily continued forward, as though she was getting everything she needed. He admired her tenacity.

And felt her pain, too, which was so not like him.

His way was to move forward, to find the answers. Had the woman really seen and heard? If so, why was she recanting?

Or had the police screwed up?

And where did they find other evidence to strengthen the case if they were going to lose this witness?

It was all there. His understanding of what was professionally at stake.

But the pain was there, too. Like he had to somehow convince Josie to give Emily what she needed so he could make the hurt go away.

Not cool.

"… I saw nothing, I heard nothing, and I can't help you."

"But you did know Lana?" Emily pressed.

"Yes."

"And you liked her?"

"Yeah."

"So why won't you help me put her killer away?"

"I…didn't see or hear anything…"

More repetition. Not normal conversation, which would more likely have included suppositions as to how the police misunderstood, or testimony to her whereabouts and how she couldn't possibly have witnessed what the police were claiming she had.

"He followed through on his threat," Emily said then,

her tone more like a defendant was on the stand. "He killed her, just like he threatened he would."

Josie looked toward the floor.

"If he walks, you can pretty much count on him doing it again. To some other sweet young woman."

Some witnesses would have buckled.

Josie didn't.

Cormac hugely disrespected her for that. For making Emily's life harder than it already was. For giving her one more thing to worry about.

And then caught himself.

Emily Hernandez was carrying his baby, but that was it. Her disappointment, her problems…they weren't his to emote over.

Other than the coming baby she wouldn't talk about, he'd taken her troubles on professionally.

Period.

It was hard enough to have an interview go so horribly wrong. But to experience such a major fail with Cormac Colton looking on? As she waited in the vacant hallway for the elevator with her pseudo bodyguard, Emily was seriously wondering what she'd done to have fate piling up the challenges all at once. She thrived on hard work, but…

Putting the phone he'd been reading back in his pocket, Cormac stared straight ahead, facing the elevator door, as he said, "NYPD has Maxwell under surveillance. He got a job as a custodian, cleaning vacant apartments, and is in Brooklyn today."

"What about an alibi for last night?"

"Said he was home all night. Surveillance didn't see him leave. But we've got someone watching your place, too, and no one saw anyone hanging around there, either. They're checking cameras in the area of both places right now."

"Maybe Maxwell guessed that I'd be staying elsewhere. He'd know that the city would take a threat against an ADA seriously."

"Which is what concerns me the most. A guy who's going to continue to up his game, to taunt you, when he knows the stakes, is either delusional or figures he has nothing to lose."

Eugene Maxwell was smart. He had run his own small but successful accounting firm before his life had imploded. And he was currently working as a custodian. Not delusional, by any means, but she could see how he might think he had nothing left to lose.

"Did they get anything on the origin of the text message I got this morning?"

Cormac shook his head. "Nothing definitive. It came from one of those internet sites that let you send texts, but getting those records is going to take a few hours, at least."

A sedated bing sounded and the door opened to an empty car.

She needed them to keep on talking business. She couldn't afford to have a single second to feel Cormac's magnetism reaching out to her in the small space.

Problem was, being turned on by him was the only good feeling in her life at the moment.

Other than…she was going to be a mother!

Maybe.

As incredible as that little plus sign appeared in her mind's eye, the vision, the knowledge was followed by incredible dread, too.

For every joy there was a corresponding shadow side, and the greater the joy, the greater the risk...

There was so much that had to happen, without fail, before she could ever hope to hold a baby of her own in her arms.

And the more she thought about the possibility that the eventuality could happen, the more afraid she became of all the things that could go wrong to prevent that from happening. And sitting in an apartment, rather than a building with people stopping by her office all day long, gave the worries far too much space to occupy.

"How does lunch in a busy diner sound before we head back to seclusion?" Cormac's tone was light as they stepped out of the elevator.

"I'd love that," she almost gushed as she grasped at the lifeline he'd just given her, thinking they'd brainstorm the Westmore case. Being with Cormac on a professional level was almost as good as knowing him sexually. Definitely the best she'd ever known.

On both counts.

And...unlike the past...they could be seen dining alone in public together since, as far as anyone knew, he'd been hired to protect her until they made an arrest on her abduction attempt.

It was odd, sitting at a table for two, facing him. He'd thrown his coat over the back of his chair before sitting, leaving her with a view of that cotton pullover covering a hard and magnificent chest and shoulders. Her gaze was like a dog on steak, and she had to continue reminding herself to look up.

Except that his eyes were focused intently on her when she did so.

They'd ordered—a burger and fries for him, cranberry

chicken salad for her—and all she could think about was how much less detrimental it was for a barely over thirty body to consume his lunch choice, than it was for a forty-three-year-old pregnant woman to do so.

If she was lucky, if all went okay, she was going to get big.

Where could she go to get professional-looking maternity wear?

No. Her mind shut down the thought as soon as it presented. She couldn't get ahead of herself. To dream of what might not be. Her heart couldn't take much more disappointment. Not if it were to remain filled with the compassion she brought to every victim, or victim's family, she interviewed.

"We need to talk about it."

Yes. Her gaze flew up to meet Cormac's and she nodded, thankful that he'd saved her from her own mental attack. "I think it's pretty obvious someone got to her," she said, watching his expression, hoping to see confirmation there. Question was, who—someone to do with Westmore, for sure—and how were they going to prove it and diffuse whatever threat was made in time to get Josie back on their side?

Cormac's frown was unexpected. Coercion had been clear…even just the way she'd held the door barely open…she'd wondered if maybe the threat was inside her apartment.

That somebody had known she was coming and had gotten to Josie first…

"The baby, Emily." His tone told her he was losing patience with her inability to discuss the child he'd fathered. Truth was, she didn't blame him.

But she'd only had a day…not even that if you considered how much of her focus had had to be on finding out who'd tried to kidnap her.

And, of course, on work.

"Obviously you're experiencing things. Thoughts. Feelings. Maybe more…"

"I told you last night, I'm still trying to wrap my mind around the whole thing." She had to lean in to be heard amidst the myriad conversations going on around them in the crowded space. Which was why she'd thought they'd just be brainstorming.

Who went to a busy city diner to discuss things you didn't want anyone to know about?

"Well, let me help you." His tone implacable, his expression resolute, she braced herself. He couldn't make her give up things before she was ready. But he certainly had the right to make his own decisions where his support of the potentially coming event, or not, was concerned.

"How are you feeling physically?" She blinked as the question came when she'd been expecting a list of his dos and don'ts. Will and won'ts.

"Fine," she said, shaking her head. "The changes inside me are so miniscule at this point that…" What did he know about the pregnancy process? He'd been six when his youngest sibling had been born. And hadn't had a serious relationship in several years. None of his siblings had kids.

"I know about the changes…and the potential schedule for them," he said, leaning back as their food was delivered. Leaving her wondering how he knew.

Surprised that he knew.

"I read through a couple of websites last night," he continued as though they hadn't been interrupted. "You could be feeling some cramping is all…"

What? They'd had glorious sex. They didn't talk personally private stuff.

And, well, she'd peed on a stick for him.

"None," she told him, taking a bite of salad she didn't want. And gave him a half smile without fully looking him in the eye.

Kinda sweet, the way he'd done that. Read up and then checked in with where she was at.

Really, really odd, too, though. She hadn't reported herself to anyone, ever. Not even the man she'd been engaged to marry.

"That's good, then." He filled his mouth with burger.

How in the hell could that be sexy?

And were they done? Cramping was the only pertinent concern at the two-month stage? She actually had not looked up the particulars.

Purposely hadn't.

Dr. Morrison would let her know all of that once they determined that the pregnancy was viable.

And then she'd read everything she could find to make certain she did everything exactly right.

Until then, no imagining, no planning…maybe some hoping…

"I want you to know that I plan to be involved. Every step of the way getting it here. And then afterward, too. And not just financially. I went through high school without a father. I'm not doing that to my kid."

He'd obviously given that one a lot of thought. And all she could do was nod.

Him with a child, as a father, she could so totally see.

Fathering her child?

Just didn't seem real.

They weren't a couple. Had never intended to be one.

And she'd long ago decided not to be a mother, too.

But in the years before she'd made that decision, she'd pictured herself married first. And welcoming the child into the family she and her husband had created.

Shaking her head, she took another bite of salad. Chewed slowly enough that the lump in her throat could pass before she needed to swallow.

"You have nothing to say to any of that?" Cormac had stopped eating. Had his arms crossed over that delicious chest.

"No."

"Nothing."

She thought about it. Shook her head. "No."

"So you aren't going to try to cut me out."

"Of course not." The words came easily, with a bit of a frown. "What good would that do anyone?"

His arms remained entwined, as though cutting her out, though. "You sure have a funny way of including me," he came back.

And she just couldn't be there for him. "I need time, Cormac." She didn't know of any other way to put it.

And to try to explain further, she'd have to delve more deeply into things she wasn't thinking about yet.

She didn't want any of it on the table. Not any of it. The potential bad or good. She needed the facts, first. But to even say that much aloud, put it on the table anyway.

"But once you've had your time, then we'll talk. And no more shutting me out. On things pertaining to the kid, only."

"Yes." She answered quickly. Because she knew that answer. Couldn't consider the "things" to which he'd referred. Or what including him would mean.

Too much.

She didn't know…

Sitting there, watching him finish his burger, absorbing his energy, she felt as though she was in some kind of dreamland, a place she couldn't stay because she didn't really belong. Not with him, at any rate.

As much as she liked him.

Cared about him, even, from a distance.

And there was one thing…

"I…would like your concession on one thing," she told him, weighing her words, sure about them.

"What's that?" He looked wary, not that she blamed him. Given their surreal and totally out-of-the-blue situation, how could either of them not be wary?

"I don't want our…situation…exposed until absolutely necessary."

He studied her. Frowned. "Define *necessary.*"

Whenever. The word came to her, along with a defensive shrug. She held them both back. Tried to express herself to him without putting anything on the damned table. "When people get suspicious."

"Of us?"

Sure. That was part of it. If she was pregnant, if she managed to continue to be, she wouldn't be able to hide changes…

"Yeah," was all she said.

"You're worried that people, our families even, will try to make us more than we are?"

There was that. But not so much. She and Cormac wanted the same things and didn't want the same things. They were both of strong minds. They'd take care of that part.

"I was twenty-one when I graduated from college. I was already involved with the man I eventually agreed to marry. I was of an age to start a family. And you were, what, ten?"

Heat washed over her. Panic ripped through her. She should have kept her mouth shut. She wasn't ready...

"You're trying to tell me you think I'm too young to do this?"

"Of course not. You're thirty-two. A lot of guys your age already have multiple kids."

"So? Your point is?" Those brown eyes bore into her, like she was an unfriendly witness on his stand.

"For almost a decade of my adult life, I'd have been committing a crime having sex with you. You know how that's going to make me look?" Did he get it at all?

How in the hell had she gotten herself into this mess? How had she let it happen?

Having wild sex with the most incredible man she'd ever met had seemed like a fabulous idea, once she'd known that she and Cormac were on the same page. She'd had her cake and eaten it, too. What did age matter when you were both just having fun?

And no one knew. There'd been no one to judge her. And now...

She could be facing what would have been the most joyous moment of her life, if they made it to that part, and, instead, even if the doctor gave her great news, she couldn't just run out and announce her bounty to the world.

People were going to be shocked. Everyone she knew, including her parents, would likely be speechless at first. And then, everyone would want to know where it had come from.

She hadn't had a date in years.

And with Cormac—a Colton, no less—insisting on involvement, she couldn't very well pass her miracle off as a product of artificial insemination by an unknown donor.

The man whose gaze she was avoiding leaned in, both arms on the table. Practically forcing her to look at him. "And you started making decisions based on other people's opinions, when?"

He didn't get it.

And she couldn't blame him. For one thing, from everything she'd heard, and from what she knew personally, no one dared question the great Cormac Colton when it came to his personal life.

Not even her.

And really, they had so many important things to worry about right now. She just needed to let it drop.

Emily smiled at Cormac, finished her salad.

And had never felt more alone in her life.

Chapter 9

Cormac had never been a sit-around type of guy. Precisely why he had chosen to be a private investigator who could call his own shots rather than a cop or a bodyguard.

With the police protection firmly in place both outside his building and on his floor whenever he left—continued threats to one of the city's star ADAs had everyone on edge—he dropped Emily back at the apartment for the series of video meetings she'd arranged with people from her office. And he gladly left her there.

Safe and secure.

And away from him.

The first thing he did was head out to Brooklyn to have a talk with Eugene Maxwell in whatever empty apartment he'd be cleaning. Cormac wasn't a cop. Didn't need a warrant. Or have to follow procedures.

Maxwell didn't have to speak to him, either.

But since Cormac had no intention of identifying himself, he figured he'd get a few words out of the guy. More importantly, he needed to see Eugene in person. To assess his size for himself, to see that, as others had told him, the guy's size and build fit the size of the man he'd seen grabbing Emily the day before. He needed to gauge if anything about him was familiar. He didn't need the guy to say a word for either of those things.

And if he could see the man's coat...

Not so much of a tell. Anyone with half a brain would ditch the coat he'd been seen wearing by a crowd of people during a failed kidnap attempt.

A call to Sean, who made a call and texted Cormac, gave him the apartment address.

The door was closed when he got there, a machine of some kind running inside. Positioning himself down the hall, out of direct sight, Cormac leaned against the wall, looking up other names from Emily's list on his phone, emailing himself pertinent articles, profiles or mentions that he came across. Just because he liked Maxwell best as the doer didn't mean that he was right.

He was leaving no stone unturned.

Nearly an hour passed. He switched shoulders against the wall. Unzipped his coat. Moved weight from one leg to the other. And kept scrolling. However long it took for his man to exit the apartment...he was up for it.

A few people passed on their way to other doors, largely ignoring him. An attractive redhead gave him a second look. He smiled at her and then returned his attention immediately to his phone, discouraging any further interaction.

He checked in with Emily a couple of times, asking

how she was doing once and how things were going the second time. Text only. Her one-word responses were the same on both occasions.

Fine.

Anytime he heard a door open, he leaned around the corner to see which one it was. By the time it was the right one, he was raring to go. He watched with quick, half-second glances, while the six-foot man in jeans and an unzipped jacket pulled a four-wheeled cart, loaded with cleaning paraphernalia and topped by a filled trash bag, out the door.

By the time Maxwell was rounding the corner toward the elevator, Cormac was standing straight, walking forward, as though he'd just arrived. He let the guy pass. But then rounded.

"Hey," he called, with a hint of question in his tone. "I'm sorry to bother you, but I'm... I never forget a face. Are you by any chance Eugene Marshall or Maxwell or something?"

The man's hesitation was accompanied by a frown before he turned back to his cart, pushing it more rapidly down the hall.

"No, wait," Cormac said as kindly as he could muster, following behind the guy, careful not to quite catch up. "I...just... I think I knew your cousin. You used to be an accountant, right?"

The man looked ordinary enough as he turned to fully face Cormac. Groomed, short dark hair. Shaved. Late forties. And he definitely fit the minimal description they had of Emily's abductor. When the attempted kidnapping had happened, Cormac hadn't noticed more than the body size. A threatening grip he had to disarm. Other than that, his gaze had been solely on Emily Hernandez, assessing her immediate health status.

"What do you want?" Eugene sounded tired more than irritated, but maybe there was a bit of both.

"It's just… I was an upstart in high school. Wanting to have my own business. Your cousin, Grant, right?" He paused, waiting for confirmation. Took the other man's stillness as such.

"Grant was helping me figure it all out. He told me to talk to you. Even took me by your office once." He named the address he'd seen in Emily's records. "But you were busy," he continued. "Grant quit coming into the sandwich shop where I worked not long after that. I figured he got that job offer he'd been hoping for. After I got enough money together to get started on my own thing, I called you, but the number was disconnected. Anyway… I just… I'd like to tell Grant thank you. I've got three shops of my own now."

Staying as vague as he possibly could, he pulled on everything he'd read about the family over the past twenty-four hours and sold it for all he was worth.

Grant had supposedly been on his way to a job interview when he'd been killed.

Eugene's implacable expression softened noticeably. He didn't come closer, but said, "You knew Grant?"

"I did." Cormac nodded, keeping his distance, playing his part. Waiting to see what Eugene would tell him. "He gave me some great advice."

Maxwell smiled. Nodded. Offered zilch. Cormac couldn't afford to just let him walk off.

Just the thought of the guy grabbing Emily had his blood boiling over, with no pot to catch it.

"So…wow, man, you had your own accounting firm. What are you doing here?" He knew how to play the fool, and to grind where the dig would sting.

"Don't ask."

"No, seriously." With a concerned gaze that nearly blinded him, Cormac took just one small step closer. Standing there looking at the man who they all pretty much knew had hurt Emily, and not being able to call for an arrest, had adrenaline pumping he didn't even know he had. "What happened? I'm doing good now. Grant helped me, maybe I can return the favor."

Shaking his head, Eugene put both hands back on his cart. But not before Cormac had seen the anger and then downright evil pass through the man's expression.

"Consider it a payback," he said then. Maxwell definitely knew what those words meant.

"Payback?" Eugene Maxwell spun around. "What do you know about payback?" The older man practically spat, fury lacing his words, though his volume was down.

"Payback's when you've had the boy you grew up with as a brother shot down for walking down the street on the way to better his life. Payback's when the thug that shot him gets off and then comes back to taunt you about it. Payback is what you do then. Payback's what happens when you finally get a break and then see your wife shacked up with the guy down the street. There's nothing you can do to get me the payback that's mine. That comes only from me."

With that, he turned, back straight, and walked proudly down the hall, turned the corner and disappeared from sight.

Good thing he didn't spin back around and see Cormac

reaching for his gun. Or notice the clenched teeth and pulse beating hard in his neck.

He couldn't arrest a guy for being bitter. But he'd never needed a man gone as badly as he did Eugene Maxwell.

The strength of his own rage took him back a couple of steps. Not out of fear for what he'd do. He knew himself better than that. But at the intensity roaring inside him.

It had the same force as the passion Emily Hernandez had raised in him, and that was absolutely not a good thing.

He definitely needed to take a breather from their situation. To put emotional distance between them while they processed their unbelievably shocking news. Emily had been right all along.

She had to try harder to explain why she wasn't able to talk to him yet. To tell him why her mind was shying away from moving forward, without actually telling him what her mind was shying away from.

How did you give understanding to things you couldn't let yourself think about? Or have a discussion about the things you couldn't discuss?

Before she could come up with any answers, she had a call from Sean Colton. "Josie Deveraux skipped on us." No introduction or "how's it going." "Her phone goes straight to a no-longer-in-service message and her super says she moved out, didn't even want her security deposit back badly enough to leave a forwarding address. She's paid up through the end of the next month, and he told her she'd have some of that money coming back, too, since they only require a thirty-day notice to vacate."

"We need to get a look at her finances," Emily said, her thoughts focused and completely on task. Thankfully, gloriously on task. "Maybe she's independently wealthy, won't miss the money and just didn't want to be bothered. Maybe she didn't have her new address yet. She could have had her stuff put into storage."

"Or maybe someone paid her off," Sean guessed, taking them where she'd been heading next.

"Exactly." And why hadn't Mitch called to let her know? "I'll call Mitch," she said then, because…protocol. He'd need to be the one to get the warrant, or she'd be stepping on toes for no good reason.

"I told him I'd call you, and get back with him," Sean said. "In light of the fact that I was going to be speaking with you anyway, because of the near abduction, and the suspicion that our cases could be related—the Evan Smith case Humphrey was going to testify on when he went missing is definitely related to you, and the threats against you also could tie into the Westmore case."

Was he stepping in as a favor to her? Because of Cormac?

She couldn't allow that. Didn't need any special favors.

Nor did she need to overreact. "Thank you," she said, then, afraid of her own emotions, went straight back to work. "I'll get to work on potential suspects," she said, explaining, "Westmore couldn't have threatened her himself. He's such a flight risk, he's not only locked up, but is being constantly monitored. So who'd do this on his behalf?"

Sean knew the case. The question wasn't only rhetorical.

"I was hoping you'd have some ideas," he told her.

"I do. Maybe someone high up on his payroll who stands to lose a way of life if Westmore's convicted. Lord knows, we haven't found anyone who actually likes the guy enough to put their neck out like this. I'll get to work on it."

They already had access to Westmore's bank accounts. She just had to follow the money.

Or come up with another source for the payout, while trying to figure out where Josie might have gone and to find a way to convince her to come back and do the right thing.

The right thing.

Like letting Sean Colton's younger brother tell the man that there was a fetus that might grow into a niece or nephew for him to love?

She was definitely a loner, but the Coltons were not. As independent as they all were personally, they were the most tight-knit, loyal family she'd ever known.

She'd never, in a million years, fit in with any of them.

But her child would.

Armed with two bags filled with individual cartons of Chinese takeout, napkins and utensils included for easy cleanup, Cormac entered the apartment just as it was getting dark. He'd have liked to have been out longer, to see for himself that Maxwell made it home, to drive by a couple of residences associated with other names on Emily's list, but the closer dusk got, the more driven he'd been to get himself back to the home front.

He wasn't just armed with dinner. He'd come in with a fully loaded mental arsenal as well. Emily could have been sitting at the table in a negligee with no underwear or with tears in her eyes, and he'd be efficient, professional and unaffected as he either covered her or found out what was wrong and tried to help fix it.

Not only did the slap of her rejection at lunch still

sting, but he'd had his own come-to-truth moment standing in that hallway in Brooklyn wanting to put a bullet into a man's back. No way he could let his emotions where anyone was concerned gain power over his mental faculties. Been there, done that.

She was in the kitchen, boiling eggs, when he came in. Looking far too at home in his personal space.

Too gorgeous and sexy and…

"I brought Chinese." He plopped the bag on the counter, didn't even think about apologizing for the gruff tone in his voice. If she thought he was pissed that she was helping herself to his food in his kitchen without even a text to say so, fine.

Better that than have her know how great she looked standing there. How, for an instant, he'd liked coming home to her in his kitchen.

"I was just boiling eggs for dinner," she said. "When I didn't hear from you…"

Her words weren't accusation. He went a little with taking them that way anyway. "I was working."

"I know. Which is why I sent out for some groceries. I just…with the baby… I feel like I should eat healthy and on a regular schedule."

Nope. No baby talk.

She'd insisted.

Too early.

But…he wanted to feed her. Or rather, to be the one to provide her sustenance. "Chinese Food is healthy."

Lame. Beneath him.

He felt like an inexperienced lout for a second there as she studied him, as though, in her greater experience, her wisdom born of age, she could see right through him, but when she nodded, he helped himself to his dinner.

He considered taking it to his room where he had less chance of thinking about her.

He wasn't some kid who had to run and hide.

Would be damned if he'd feel like a hostage in his own home.

Pulling out a chair a little more roughly than maybe necessary, he sat at the end of the table, where Sean had been the day before, and started in before she'd joined him.

They were both eating because they needed the nourishment and the food was there and hot. They were not having dinner together.

Because, like it or not, she'd been right at lunch. The eleven years between them…he might not notice them, or care. They might not matter a whit to him when he thought of her, looked at her, talked to her, even. But they clearly mattered to her. And probably would to some others, too.

He'd been ten when she graduated from college. If he'd have been there, if they'd known each other, she'd likely have smiled at him, given him a sweet, little-boy hug, and forgotten his existence.

And he probably would have squirmed and thought her hug was gross.

At ten, he'd thought pretty much all females were mushy and gross. Except Eva, of course. She'd been four and pretty sassy and cute as he remembered it. Except when she got in his stuff. That pissed him off. But she'd made him laugh with her fantasy-mixed logic and assertions.

"I want to apologize for my closed-mindedness at lunch." Her words hit him before she'd even settled in her seat.

He shook them off. "No need," he told her, stuffing more food in his mouth, using the fact that he was eating with chopsticks, to keep his hand there, holding the noodles in. And his head angled. So he couldn't look over at her.

He chewed, swallowed, to her stillness.

"I talked to Sean," he said, going for another bite, still without looking at her directly. His food gave him something to focus on and he was smart enough to take the assistance.

"Then you know Josie's gone." Finally. She'd settled into her chair. Was taking a bite of food.

Peripheral vision was a bitch. Giving him sights he really didn't need.

Those lips...noticing them just led to other things, which led to more, which shot him over to Brooklyn wanting a man dead without just cause.

"I know," he said, swallowing the oversize bite he'd shoved in as she sat down.

She talked about the money trail. The work she'd done since Sean's call. With nothing to report yet.

"I know Wes is behind it," she said then, the anger in her tone finding comradery with that still seething within him. "Just like we all know he killed Lana. I'll be damned if he gets away with it."

And there. He was back on track. "Just like we're convinced that Eugene Maxwell is out to get you, and we just can't prove it," he said. Common ground. Professional ground.

Cramming himself in the small space they'd just created, he ate and replayed for her his conversation with the loving-cousin-and-husband-accountant turned murderer.

"You think he figured out you were sniffing around?"

she asked, reminding him of the first night they'd worked late. It had been all about the case, and he'd still been lit up. Even just talking business with her. What in the hell was it about her?

Cormac shrugged. "My guess is no, but, as you said before, he's a smart man. But he's also completely filled with rage, and I don't see him stopping until he's had every ounce of payback he can get."

When she shuddered, he shut up.

As usual, when it came to her, he'd gone too far.

Gathering up his empty cartons, he told Emily he had calls to make and went to his room, leaving her to spend the evening at the table alone.

Chapter 10

Wow.

Sitting alone with half-empty food cartons and no appetite, Emily stared down the hall where Cormac's retreating back had just been.

She could say one thing for the man. He was consistent.

All in and then gone.

He'd been all up in her business, and then, when she'd listened and realized he was right, he'd retreated from her completely. Wouldn't even give her a chance.

Just as he'd done two months before.

Completely into her. And then…not.

Even with boundaries established between them, to protect his personal needs as well as hers, she couldn't count on him to hang around.

Good to know.

Hard.

But good. As she'd originally thought and continued

to tell herself, she was going to be doing the baby thing on her own. She couldn't keep him from visiting his child, of course, nor would she want to, but in terms of the hard stuff, the daily grind, the life—she most certainly couldn't count on him.

Or let her child do so.

Knowing that going in would make things a whole lot less painful in the long run.

She slept surprisingly well, for the second night in a row. Waking up on Wednesday morning, she was shocked to see the sun shining through the blinds in Cormac's spare bedroom. Why on earth, how on earth, with everything going wrong, with her life at stake, could she just drift off and rest?

The idea that it might be because she was at Cormac's house, that she somehow felt safe and taken care of with him, had her flying out of bed and into the shower.

It wasn't Cormac's presence or home that was inducing sleep. It couldn't be. But the pregnancy...that made more sense. Her body might not look or feel any differently yet, but the life was there inside her. Miniscule, yes, but growing. Feeding off her energy.

Of course, she'd sleep differently.

It would be the same if she was at home, too. Or anywhere else.

After her shower—and a quick, normal check-in call with her parents, telling them she was fine, hearing about their recent day cruise—she dressed in tight-fitting black flex pants and matching tapered jacket with a long-sleeved white tee underneath, zipped up her ankle boots, feeling glad that she'd at least gotten the restful night thing settled. And, with her mind on getting through the day one step at a time, she went out to see what Cormac was up to.

Only to find a note on the table, letting her know that he'd be gone most of the morning, following up on Blake Nygren and Julius Hemming, the other two men on her list of recently released convicts she'd prosecuted who raised the most fear in her.

Preliminary reports had already been pulled on both of them. Sean had spoken to their parole officers himself. He'd spoken to Eugene Maxwell's, too.

While there was nothing that allowed police to arrest any of the three, there'd been nothing to definitively rule out any of them, either.

They all could have appeared basically the same size, with overcoats and hoods considered, and none of them had provable alibis for late Monday morning. Julius Hemming claimed to have been in a cab on his way to a comic shop, but said he'd used a private cab and paid cash, and no one had been able to verify if he had or not. The comic shop, not far from the courthouse and Emily's office, had been closed due to a flooded bathroom.

And Blake Nygren said he'd been in Atlantic City, gambling, but couldn't remember which casinos he'd played in. So far, no video surveillance had turned up to prove he'd been there.

Cormac texted while she was still brewing the decaffeinated tea she'd had delivered as part of her grocery order the day before. The texts sent to her phone were a dead end.

They'd been sent through the internet, as already known. The source appeared to be a computer registered to a dead man with no known connections to any of their suspects, using free Wi-Fi by the courthouse.

The kind of thing an accountant could figure out, she texted back.

Any of them could have learned computer skills inside.

She'd just been thinking the same when his message came through. And with that moment of common ground, and the flood of warmth that accompanied it, she considered telling him about the doctor appointment she had that morning. Then, remembering the night before, she chose not to do so.

Best to find out what she was dealing with first.

If the pregnancy wasn't viable, there'd be no more need for anything but professional discussion between them. And she could put her one-time fascination for, and association with, a much younger man down in the "what was I thinking" category.

Cormac found Julius Hemming sitting on a stoop, without a coat, smoking a cigarette. He had already been by Maxwell's place twice and had checked in with the officers watching the guy, and the bitter man hadn't done a single thing they could arrest him for. Cormac was not in the best of moods.

The second near sleepless night he'd just spent wasn't helping matters. With the gorgeous, sexy woman sleeping with his baby inside her just down the hall, he dozed, and kept waking with the sense that he should be crawling into bed beside her. Holding her. As he'd done for one pretty spectacular week…

Hemming admitted having threatened the…woman… who'd prosecuted him, though his word choice hadn't started out that congenial. He'd barely gotten the *B* sound out of his mouth before Cormac had stepped in, only as a warning, but the other man didn't know that.

"You guys just don't let up, do ya?" the man continued,

taking a long drag. "First the cops are asking me to prove my whereabouts, and now they're sending thugs to talk to me?" His breath came out in a puff of smoke.

Not the smartest man on the block, for sure, saying that with said thug standing over him. But Cormac wasn't interested in the man enough to point out the obvious lack. He'd noticed the way the guy's right arm only lifted halfway to take a puff from his smoke.

"You hurt your arm, *Juleeuss*?" he asked, drawing out the word. He could see his own breath, too, but his was clean.

"A fight on the block. My second week in. The other guy was hurtin' worse."

And there you had it.

No way that man had used that arm to haul Emily up against him the other morning. He didn't figure the guy had enough brain cells left to know how to send untraceable text messages, either, but saw no reason to belabor the matter.

Warning the guy to watch his step, Cormac turned to go.

"Hey," Julius called out.

Swinging on his heel, Cormac turned back.

"No way I'm going back there," the man said. "That's why I'm not making no one pay for nothin'."

With a nod, Cormac hailed the cab coming up the block.

And when the driver asked, "Where to?" he actually hesitated, thinking about dropping by his place just to see Emily for a few minutes.

For…no good reason.

Blake Nygren was meeting with his parole officer, so no reason to go there.

But Cormac had other responsibilities. Legitimate ones. Pressing ones.

He gave the cab driver the Kellys' address.

Humphrey's young wife, Ciara, had texted that she would be home all morning and he needed to get Humphrey's laptop.

With a quick call he arranged to have one of the department's electronics-sniffing K-9 dogs, Bing, meet him there as well. Bing was a whiz at finding thumb drives and even if they were ending up with confidential client records, the team was going to do what it had to do to find Humphrey.

After showing them to Humphrey's office, Ciara excused herself to let them do whatever they needed to do, telling them the dog was welcome to investigate the entire place. Cormac still wasn't sure how he felt about Ciara, who'd married Humphrey after a whirlwind courtship. For a while he thought she might have had some role in Humphrey's disappearance. But now he and his siblings all believed that the distress she was showing over Humphrey's absence was real.

It didn't take long for Cormac to figure out that he wasn't going to find anything in Humphrey and Ciara's apartment. No computer, or drives. And no phone, hidden anywhere, either. He called in Forensics, but, as he'd suspected after only a glance, Humphrey's home office had been wiped clean.

The same was true at Humphrey's Fifth Avenue office.

"I don't know why he'd have taken his computer with him to court, but I suppose he could have," Cormac told Sean on the phone as he headed back for another check on Eugene Maxwell. The man was supposed to be in a Manhattan apartment building from late morning until midafternoon. "We can assume Humphrey had his phone on him."

"Knowing Humphrey, he'd take the laptop, with the recorded file of his interview with the defendant, just in case," Sean agreed. "And since a laptop wasn't found in the janitor's closet, or anywhere else around the courthouse, we can hope that he's got the laptop with him." During their preliminary investigation, they'd discovered signs of a struggle inside the utility closet at the courthouse, but they hadn't been able to find any video or confirm a connection to Humphrey.

Where was Humphrey? Cormac wondered, not for the first time, how his uncle could have vanished without leaving a trace.

"I'll have someone run a check on pawnshops," Sean continued. "Just in case." And then added, "By the way, I also checked up on our old friend Wes Westmore. There's no evidence of an obvious payout from Westmore's account to Josie Devereaux. I'm seeing this more like a threat, than buying her off."

Yeah, so was Cormac, and the threat theory was way worse. Someone like Josie could probably be convinced to give up the money, but if she feared so badly for her life that she'd rushed out of town, chances weren't good that anything was going to convince her to turn around and come back.

If they could even find her.

"And if Westmore holds the power to threaten lives, then maybe he's behind the attack on Emily?" he said aloud, a strike of cold fear slicing through him.

What the hell? He didn't fear.

Not for clients.

But for his kid?

"Doesn't seem likely." Sean's answer pulled his head out of the muck. "They'll just replace her with another ADA."

Yeah, they'd already determined that. But… "Unless she's onto something that no one else has figured out yet."

He had to get home. Get Emily to talk to him.

Better yet, he'd ask her out to lunch. She'd said more in the diner the day before then at any other time he'd tried to get her to open up to him.

He hadn't liked what he'd heard.

But he didn't have to like Emily's thoughts, or feelings. Her theories or her suppositions. He just had to know what they were, as they pertained to him and the cases they were working, so he could keep her safe.

And so that he could figure out what being a father to her child was going to mean for him.

An entire swarm of overactive butterflies had taken up residence in Emily's stomach. The text from Cormac, asking her to meet him for lunch halfway between his place and Brooklyn, added a nest of hornets in there, too.

Or maybe she was just too focused on her insides to deal with reality.

Alone in the small patient room, waiting for Dr. Morrison to come back for a chat once she'd read through the urinalysis and blood test results, she was about to tell Cormac she couldn't make it, until he texted a second time to tell her that he'd come back to the apartment if she preferred.

No. She didn't want that. She was closer to the midway meeting place than she was to his apartment. She sent a quick text to her police escort out in the waiting room, to make certain that the woman wasn't due to switch shifts or something before lunch. She'd barely heard back and was just hitting Send on the text to Cormac, letting him know they'd be there, and setting the time for half an hour later than he'd suggested, when the patient room door opened.

Her stomach plummeted and her heart beat double time. *Please, let my baby be fine.* Until that moment she hadn't realized that somehow, in the past couple of days, her whole life, her happiness, her future, was wrapped up in that one small sentence.

Age differences, attractions, work…none of it mattered in that moment.

Only…

"Everything looks good." Dr. Morrison was still pulling her stool over toward the chair in which Emily had plopped herself after getting dressed. But Emily knew the exact second when the doctor got a look at her face.

At the tears streaming down her cheeks.

She felt Dr. Morrison's hand on her own, in her lap. "I'm assuming these are happy tears?"

"Yes." She tried to smile. Hiccupped, instead. "I apologize…" She tried for a deep breath. Managed a shaky one. "I just…wouldn't let myself hope… I mean…look at me… I'm forty-three…" All the breaths in between the words weren't enough to fill her lungs.

She was going to be a mother! A mother! With a baby!

As ludicrous as the idea seemed, the child inside her was suddenly more real to Emily than anything else in her life had ever been.

Dr. Morrison let go of Emily's hand to open the file she'd carried over with her, and Emily's palm slid over to rest against her own completely flat belly.

It was real. A tiny little life was growing in there…

"I've got several pamphlets here for you," the doctor was saying, handing them over one by one as she talked about diet and exercise, about extra ultrasound appointments and things they'd watch due to Emily's age. But she was smiling as she said, "I want you to schedule the first sonogram as you leave, first available, so we can listen to the heartbeat, and get measurements…"

Heartbeat! "You can hear that this soon?"

"Between two and three months, yes." The woman who practiced both obstetrics and gynecology and had been Emily's doctor for years, smiled again, telling Emily about physiological changes that would occur, changes that the doctor had noticed, during her internal exam, that had already occurred. Dr. Morrison also noted the lack of any sign of bleeding or infection, and said again that all looked and felt perfectly healthy.

Emily hung on every word, couldn't wipe the trembling smile off her lips, and finally let out a deep breath.

"Is the father in the picture?" the doctor asked then, meeting Emily's gaze with concern.

In all the years she'd been Dr. Morrison's patient, she'd never had a man "in the picture."

"Yes," she said, looking away.

"Have you told him yet?"

"Yes." There was more to the question.

Emily didn't have the answers to give the woman.

"If he wants to be involved, if you want him to be at this point, he's welcome to join you for the ultrasound," the doctor said then, not pressing.

But she had to be wondering, Emily surmised.

Dying of curiosity. Who had the workaholic ADA hooked up with, at forty-three, to have a baby?

Another fortysomething whose sperm might be a little less reliable, just as her eggs could have been?

Could still be, she amended as Dr. Morrison handed her the last pamphlet. Something about giving birth over forty.

There'd be genetic tests. Some birth conditions were more prevalent when a woman reached a certain age.

So much to think about. To consider. To worry about.

To hide, at least for the moment, as she slid the pamphlet into her satchel and went out to join her police escort for the trip across town. Officer Donovan. Sheila, she'd said.

The woman was nice, in her thirties and circumspect. She hadn't asked any questions when Emily had told her she had a doctor's appointment that morning.

And because the office serviced women of all ages, Emily wasn't concerned that the police officer would draw any conclusions she didn't want drawn.

No way the younger woman was going to think her past forty and very single charge was having a baby.

For the moment, Emily needed it that way.

And in that moment, with the doctor's last pamphlet riding along in her satchel, she felt very much alone, too.

Alone with her child.

So…not so alone.

If she was able to successfully birth the baby, she was never going to be a family of one again.

Chapter 11

The diner he'd chosen, one he frequented with his siblings, had a wait. And no room to wait inside. No way he was having the woman pregnant with his child standing outside in the cold.

"Let's head down to Leonardo's," he suggested. The place was on two floors, had space between the tables, wasn't a current trendy hot spot, and, because it was more expensive, wouldn't be swarming with crowds of impatient hungry people. "You like Italian, and they make some of the best scampi I've ever had," he continued, feeling a bit...nervous...as he ushered her down the walk. "I discovered the place when I was doing a job for the FBI, and you can always get a table. Until a million other people find it."

He was chattering like a kid.

She just...seeing her walk up in those ankle boots, in her sleek business attire, with her long, dark wavy hair

flowing over the shoulders of her coat, and those lips…
he thought about her carrying his child and felt like he
had to be doing something.

Doing more.

"You sounded like you had something you needed
to talk about," she said, as she walked beside him, her
shoulders a bit hunched inward with the cold. He could
see her breath when she spoke and had the ridiculous
urge to open his mouth and catch the air. To suck it in.

Like a kiss. The thought was fleeting. There and gone,
as he kept her between the buildings they were passing
and the street, kept a hand at her back, and watched all
doorways they passed.

Overkill, maybe.

At the moment, all suspects were occupied elsewhere.
Unless it was the Westmore thing…

"I do need to talk," he told her then, "once we get inside."

As though understanding that he needed to keep his
focus on their surroundings right now, she remained silent, pushing his pace a bit, like she didn't need him
slowing his stride on her account.

Until, just before they reached the restaurant, her step
faltered.

His arm automatically tightened around her; all he
could think of was keeping her with him, covering her,
shoving her into a safe place before reaching for his gun.
Then he glanced in the direction she'd been looking…
and faltered, too.

He slowed to a brief stop as he stared in the window
that had snagged her attention to the point of missing
her step.

The Baby Shop. Right next door to Leonardo's. All
the times he'd been to the place, he'd never noticed, or

mentally cataloged at least, the kind of retail shop right next door.

He'd known there was a store there, but…

Cribs and cradles, chairs and swingy things…

His gaze took them in while his mind blipped for a second.

When he felt Emily move again, he was right there with her. He checked around them, getting her inside the restaurant as quickly as he could.

She glanced at him as they stood behind a couple of men who'd entered right before them. And then she said, "That stuff is a long ways off," as though reassuring him.

Or herself?

Had his face borne the shock he was feeling inside?

He was going to be a father.

Wrapping his mind around that just wasn't easy.

Or happening fast.

Cormac was all business during lunch. It was as though seeing the baby things she'd be needing—maybe even the fact that she'd paused for a second to look at them, to marvel at the reality that she was probably going to be needing one of everything she saw—had built yet another wall between them.

Since she hadn't wanted to talk to him about the morning's visit until she'd had time to process, to read the pamphlets, to have a clear plan for presenting the information, she welcomed his keeping conversation all business.

Until it occurred to her that maybe, after the night before, business was all she and Cormac were ever going to give each other.

Was he really going to walk out on her and the baby?

For good?

Shards of panic shot through her. She'd just told Dr. Morrison that the father would be in the picture.

Why had she done that when Cormac had made it clear that he was bolting again?

How was she...could she...what if she needed bed rest? How would she...?

She would. Just like always.

Life had sent her challenges before. Ones without the glorious bounty this one brought with it. She'd handled every one of them.

She'd find a way.

Starting with focusing on work until she was alone. She was glad to hear that Julius Hemming was no longer a suspect. The way the man had threatened her had kept him at the top of her list, just behind Maxwell.

Having him gone seemed like a weight being lifted off her.

"I'm still liking Maxwell first and foremost," Cormac said as he dug into his bowl of shrimp scampi. She'd gone for the classic lasagna. Not a choice she'd normally make, most particularly at lunch, but it had sounded good to her.

And it was tasting fantastic.

Starting that night, her diet was going to be strictly guided by whatever the pamphlet in her satchel told her.

"But we need to talk about Westmore."

Watching his eyes as he spoke, the depth of mental focus those dark orbs portrayed, Emily caught her breath for a second. Cormac's vibrancy, his dedication to his life's calling, captivated her as much that afternoon as it had the first time she'd met him.

He was smart, yes, but so were a lot of guys. With Cormac, there was more. Layers of more.

"Is something wrong?" She'd been staring at him. He was looking right back at her. Gazes locked. As she recognized the concerned frown overtaking his expression, she blinked.

She cut off another small bite of her layered pasta. "No," she told him. "Is there something specific you need from the Westmore case?"

She wasn't sure what that had to do with her stalker. They'd already determined that, for all intents and purposes, she was just a placeholder there. Pick her off and another ADA would just step in. It was how the system worked.

She made herself look over at him again, as she chewed the small bite. She challenged herself to look without getting lost.

Cormac told her that if, as they suspected, Josie Devereaux hadn't been paid off, but threatened, that maybe Emily *was* a Westmore target. Not as the prosecutor, but for something she was onto as she built her case.

"Something that another ADA wouldn't yet have access to, something that's just brewing for you," he explained. "You're known for coming up with arguments that no one else has thought of, for seeing small truths in evidence that no one else sees, putting pieces together in a way no one else would have done."

She'd built a reputation over the years. She won more cases than most of her peers. It just meant she was good at what she did.

Because she truly loved what she did. Prosecuting criminals, getting them off the streets, wasn't just a job to her.

It was a calling.

Just like Cormac's investigative work was for him.

That was another part of what had first attracted them to each other…

She almost spaced out in his gaze again. She gave her head a little shake. "You want to know my working theories," she summarized, getting herself back on track.

"Yeah."

And so she gave them to him. Cleanly. Distinctly. Building from Westmore's egotistical, entitled personality and attitude, what they knew of his homelife growing up, and ending with, "My thought is that he can't help himself. I was planning to get a psych eval, expecting it to come back as narcissistic personality. Beyond that, I was thinking about building a case based on Westmore's true belief that he deserved to have whatever he wanted, by showing a history of things he's wanted and how he obtained them."

It was all just an idea…in the thinking stage…it might never come to be anything at all. It was how all her cases started out.

Her getting inside a defendant's head.

"Looking for the bottom-line truths that led to the crime," Cormac said.

And with a two-month flashback, she remembered him. Them. "Yes," she said. He'd gotten her from the beginning. Thought like her, sometimes.

They'd been two professional minds on the same wavelength.

Equals. The same in every way that mattered to their associations. Both business and pleasure.

They'd made sense.

But a thirty-two-year-old successful hunk with enough energy to move mountains and a forty-three-year-old starting-to-show-wrinkles-around-her-eyes prosecutor—

one who had to take extra precautions and get extra rest to even have a chance of producing a healthy baby—having a baby together?

That didn't make sense to her.

At all.

It was like the pregnancy had stopped her in her tracks, while he still had miles and miles ahead of him to travel.

Cormac paid for lunch. They were heading home—his home, where she was staying—to research Westmore. Articles about him, social media accounts detailing his exploits, anything they could find that would help build the picture Emily needed.

And while they were at it, Cormac was going to be making a list of anyone who popped out as a possible patsy for Westmore. Someone who'd issue threats and appear alarming enough to strike terror within his target.

He and Emily were thriving again, doing together what they did so well—work. When they were on a job, the boundaries were clear and, with that understanding, he'd never enjoyed being with another person more.

He was just waiting for her to come back from the restaurant's restroom when Sean called. There'd been a possible sighting of Humphrey and the team had to get down there as soon as possible. By the time Emily came toward him, her police escort was already pulling up outside.

"I've got to get over to Amsterdam and 116th," he told her, hating to leave her, yet beyond anxious to get on the streets to look for his uncle.

"By Columbia?" she asked. "I graduated from there.

"A psychiatrist in a university setting makes sense if he's working on something," she added, all while he stood there wanting her to show at least a modicum of regret that he wouldn't be accompanying her back to his place as planned.

The feeling passed in seconds. As soon as Emily's escort was by her side, adrenaline pushed Cormac into a cab, and by the time he jumped out, joining Sean, Eva and Liam, he'd let go of the emotional lapse. Reactions like those were why he didn't get involved in deep, committed interpersonal relationships outside his family.

"A former patient of Humphrey's, Rob Widdicombe, heard about his disappearance on the news and called 911 just a little bit ago, saying he saw Humphrey walking down this block—" Sean pointed up and back from where they were standing "—arm in arm with a woman."

"A woman?" Eva asked, clearly taken aback.

"With his young new wife at home?" Liam said what Cormac was thinking.

"Humphrey wasn't a philanderer even when he wasn't in a relationship." Eva shook her head.

"This guy, Widdicombe, said that Humphrey had a black mustache, black plastic-framed glasses and a Russian fur hat on—"

"There you go." Cormac's system deflated as he realized he'd left Emily and raced across town for nothing. "It wasn't even him."

And any hope he'd been holding that they were about to find Humphrey alive and well, faded.

"That's what I thought," Sean said, a definite note of urgency in his tone. "Which is why I called Widdicombe myself. He sounded damned convincing, guys. He says he spent months with Humphrey. That Humphrey saved his life. He'd know him anywhere. We need to split up.

Scour the area, talk to store owners, clerks, see if anyone else saw him."

Because he respected his brother's detective skills, his cop's gut, as much as anything else, Cormac jogged toward the area Sean gave him, stopping in every doorway, phone in hand to show Humphrey's picture. Describing the mustache, black plastic glasses and Russian-style fur hat. He questioned every owner, clerk and janitor he saw. Every bystander.

And an hour later, he met back up with his siblings, frustrated as hell. "I got a couple of people who saw a tall man in a Russian hat, but they didn't get a good look at him," he reported in just as Liam was walking up.

"Same here," his twin added as Eva and Sean both nodded.

His siblings all had their jackets unzipped, as his own was. Their cheeks were pink, probably from the cold, but it was the disappointment in their gazes that got to him.

Widdicombe had been sure enough to convince a seasoned detective like Sean, there had to be something to that.

"Obviously, it wasn't Humphrey," his brother was saying. "Sorry for dragging you all down here when we've all got so much to do."

"Humphrey would have gotten in touch with one of us if he was okay. He wouldn't just be walking around town arm in arm with some woman…" Liam's lips were tight as his words fell off.

Like they got sometimes when his twin was holding back stronger emotion.

"I agree with Liam," Eva added, jumping from foot to foot as she rezipped her department jacket. "No way he wouldn't call one of us if he was able."

But the only contact they'd had from Humphrey in all this time was one brief sounding of the alarm on his watch. And that had been a month ago.

They were preparing themselves for the bad news. Cormac got it. Just as he knew he was already prepared for the worst.

But something wasn't sitting right with him. Humphrey had saved Widdicombe's life. A guy didn't forget something like that.

Didn't forget the face he'd stared at, hour after hour, the words he'd obviously clung to, as he'd fought for and won his emotional and mental freedom.

Just as some guys couldn't let go of a need for payback when someone cost them their freedom.

He couldn't explain Humphrey on the arm of another woman, leaving his new bride, Ciara, at home, and all of them, worried sick about him.

But he'd learned over the years not to take anything at face value. If someone was threatening Humphrey, or his family—Ciara and the Coltons—the psychiatrist would stay out of touch. Maybe even adopt a disguise.

There could be another explanation, too. Humphrey could have joined in with one of his seedier patients and gotten himself into something he didn't want any of them to know about.

Cormac didn't believe this was a possibility. But then, when he loved someone, he went blind to their truths. Which meant his siblings were probably right about Humphrey. The patient was wrong. And Humphrey was gone.

He was going to have to tell Emily about his lapse in judgment so she'd protect the baby from it. She couldn't rely on Cormac to see or know if the kid got into something bad.

Love blinded him.

Which was why he was never ever going to hook up, adult to adult, again.

And with the kid? Emily would be there for protection, to fill in Cormac's lapses.

Getting into a cab to head back to his place, he knew that the reminder couldn't have come at a better time.

Chapter 12

Emily needed to get home. Staying at Cormac's had seemed necessary, but they'd gone twenty-four hours without a threat, which made sense, since Maxwell knew he was being watched. Yes, the ex-con likely knew where she lived, but with the police watching her place outside, the doorman downstairs and her triple locks, she should be fine.

She couldn't just keep sitting at Cormac's dining table, fighting thoughts of him. The only way to regain control of her life was to get away from the constant reminders of what wasn't going to be.

She had to look at her space in terms of the rearranging she was going to have do, rather than just thinking and guessing. Needed to measure, to figure out which room would work best as a nursery—probably her office—and figure out where things would go.

Unless, what if she ended up with a live-in nanny?

Where would her office go?

The dining room was out—there was no way to close the door on the noise that might be coming from a child and nanny playing when she worked from home during the day.

A nanny.

Where would she find one? A person who she'd be able to trust with her life—her baby's life—seemed like an impossibly tall order to her, but she knew that people all over the city had them.

Thankfully, having a good job, having worked it for two decades, having lived alone all that time and taken few vacations, she had no financial worries.

Could she risk her baby's life on the say-so and vetting of a service where people were being paid to do jobs, without personal stake in the outcome?

No way. Her days were filled with people others had trusted, who'd done horrible things for their own gain.

Businesses and individuals alike…

Chest tight, she stared at her computer screen. How could she bring a baby into a world that…

…had people like her who dedicated their lives to trying to do the right thing and make the world a better place.

And it wasn't just her.

There were far more people who cared and did good than the opposite. Just because her days were filled with the opposite didn't mean her baby was destined to…

What?

She'd met plenty of great people throughout her career.

Like the Coltons. The family gave their lives to serving the people of New York City. To keeping them safe.

Look how they'd piled on for her! Other than that brief

week with Cormac, and a couple of cases with Sean, she was a complete stranger to them.

Albeit one who was carrying their biology in her body.

Not that they knew that, of course.

Other than Cormac.

Who continued to pull at her, to consume her thoughts, even though she knew that they were meant to be apart.

Needed to be apart.

She had to get home. She had to get back to her own life and quit worrying about having had sex with a man more than a decade her junior…

Emily was still sitting at the table, her thoughts going around in circles with no clear answers except a need to escape, when Cormac texted to say he was on his way up.

He must not have found Humphrey. Surely he'd have texted to let her know if they had him.

Sliding the pregnancy pamphlets spread on the table back into her purse, she reminded herself to act her age and was prepared to discuss business. Most particularly, she was eager to hear what was going on with Humphrey, to escape into the world she and Cormac legitimately inhabited together, when she heard Cormac's key in the lock.

He had barely finished giving her the rundown on his disappointing afternoon search when she blurted, "I'd like to head back to my place."

"You need to pick up more things? I can send someone." Pulling out his phone, he came closer and said, "I'll call Eva."

"No!" She hadn't meant to speak so sharply. Or, really, to speak of leaving at all, until they'd had more of a discussion about the immediate personal future that, ready or not, they both had a part in. But the second he'd walked in the door, she'd started waffling again.

The whole possible bed-rest thing.

"I want to go home."

She needed him to refuse to let her go. To insist that it wasn't safe. To list all of the reasons why it was a bad idea.

And…

She also needed him to tell her that he agreed it was time for her to go back to her place. To mention that there'd been no threats for twenty-four hours and Maxwell was under watch. Maybe even throw in the bit about Julius Hemming being off their list.

She needed him to engage with her on the topic.

She needed him to be Cormac and state things logically, unemotionally, so she could be her corresponding self and get on with things. She needed him to be the man she'd known and bring out the best in her just as he'd done two months before.

Instead, Cormac dropped to the chair at the end of the table.

And just sat.

So many things needed to be said. Some of which weren't his to say. Needing to chase a suspect, catch him and then…maybe chase another, Cormac sat at his dining table, at a loss.

He'd looked over the file being shared by everyone working Emily's attempted abduction in the cab on the way back from Morningside Heights. The police escort report said she'd gone out that morning to an undisclosed location. The outing had taken from midmorning until she'd met him for lunch.

She'd come straight to him from there and hadn't given even a hint of indication that she hadn't just come from his place.

She'd been working on her own abduction. He'd figured that out immediately. After all, it's what he'd have done.

Whatever she'd come up with after he'd left that morning—or maybe even the night before for all he knew since he got up and left the apartment before she'd come out of her room—she'd followed up with on her own.

Meaning she didn't trust him?

Didn't want him involved?

Hadn't wanted to fight him for the right to do things on her own?

As independent as she was, maybe she hadn't even given a thought to telling him.

How the hell did he know?

Or, for that matter, how did he discern, in the midst of their bizarre situation, what was even right?

Yeah, she could have just gotten herself killed.

He could have, too, meeting with Maxwell. With Hemming. It was all part of the job.

His job, not hers.

Prosecutors weren't usually directly in the line of danger.

He was legally armed, licensed and trained.

She was not. She didn't even carry a gun.

"Are you aware that your police escort logs time in and out every time you leave this apartment?"

Eyes wide, her gaze landed on him, very briefly, before gluing to her computer screen. "No."

If the situation hadn't been so serious, and he hadn't

been fighting desperation in his dealings with her, he might have smiled at the truculent tone in her voice.

Like she was in trouble. And worried about what her punishment would be.

He'd like to punish her all right. With soft touches all over that sweet body of hers. With tender kisses and…

Where was the tenderness thing coming from?

There hadn't been a lot of tenderness between them during their physical encounters. Mostly they'd been hunger-fueled, sweaty workouts.

Shaking his head, he asked, "Since I'm working the case and doing my best to keep you safe, do you mind telling me where you were? I assume you were following a lead, as you have every right to do, and you followed protocol by taking your escort with you, I just…"

Was hurt that she hadn't kept him in the loop.

And that was just damned ludicrous.

"I was at the ob-gyn."

Oh. *Ohhhhh.*

"She did an internal and everything looks good. Changes that happen are happening. There's no sign of bleeding or infection."

Cormac froze. He appreciated her businesslike tone. Nevertheless, his heart was pounding like a kettle drum in his chest.

"I'm considered high risk, due to my age, and will need closer monitoring. She wants me to get a blood pressure cuff and take regular readings as I'll be more prone to preeclampsia."

"Preeclampsia?" Throat dry, he held back the cough that needed to accompany the word. He wanted to sound as calm and in control as she was.

She'd come straight to lunch with him after this appointment and…he hadn't noticed anything different about her.

Because she was that good at hiding things? Was taking it all so much better in stride than he was?

Or because he'd been too busy building walls between them so he didn't fall for her that he hadn't allowed himself to notice her as anything more than a work associate across the lunch table?

"It's a condition that occurs during pregnancy sometimes when the expectant mother's blood pressure soars to dangerous levels. If it's not caught, it can be fatal."

"And if it's caught?"

"As long as it's treated, mother and baby can be just fine. And, apparently, after the birth, the mother's blood pressure generally returns to normal and there are no lasting effects."

He pulled out his phone and opened his favorite shopping app. He typed in blood pressure cuff, tapped the one with the highest rating and tapped once more for an instant buy.

"Cormac?"

Shaking her head, she was staring at him, mouth open. And then, when she had his attention, asked, "Are you even listening to me?"

"Of course. The doctor-recommended Heart-Healthy Supreme Cuff will be arriving tomorrow."

Eyebrows raising, she blinked.

She didn't smile.

But she didn't look angry, either.

"Go on," he told her. He was ready to take mental notes, ferret out any action he could take to make things easier on her.

She talked about diet. Fine, he'd put himself in charge of that.

If she'd let him.

He could deliver to her place or his. Either way, that one he could get done even with a full day of work.

When she said she was going to need extra rest, that she'd likely be getting more tired within the next month or two, he panicked a little.

Emily wasn't going to agree to slow down.

Any more than he would. You powered through.

She was starting on a vitamin regimen immediately. "She wants me to have extra ultrasound checks, at least in the beginning," she told him next. "And recommended that I have an amniocentesis, too."

He looked that one up. He could feel her watching him. He wasn't fond of the words on the screen. There was risk. The needle wasn't little. Would likely hurt her.

"There's a higher risk of Down syndrome," he read aloud. There were other possible defects, too. Potential complications that the invasive test would detect.

"The amnio thing…it's like good investigative work," he said aloud. "To show us what dangers we might be facing, yes, but more to rule out suspects. Like Hemming. We don't have to bother sending any energy in his direction anymore."

Emily's smile shocked his entire system. Left fire burning in his veins. And then she sobered.

"There's a higher-than-normal chance that toward the end, I could need to be on bed rest." Her words didn't put out the fire. It just shifted the hottest point of the blaze from his groin to his gut section.

"My uterine wall isn't twenty anymore. It might thicken

as well as it would have when I was twenty. Or it might not."

"Can they give you drugs to help with that?"

"They can do things, yes, but it's not just the uterus. It's everything else, too."

The intent look in her dark brown eyes hit him in the chest. What a chump he was, thinking about how being a father was going to affect his life. Trying to figure out where Emily would fit in. Big-picture things. While she'd been dealing with real-life, potentially life-threatening facts. Like, she was in her forties, not her twenties, producing another life.

"You still want to have the baby?" he asked, no judgment, or even his own opinion, at all present.

"More than anything in the world." Her tone…almost angelic…set him back in his chair. Tightened the band around his chest some more.

"What does your doctor say? Did she recommend that you think about not having it?"

"That wasn't even mentioned," she said, frowning now. "She said I'm in excellent shape, and that I have every chance of having a healthy baby. Look, Cormac, if you're having second thoughts…if you don't want the baby… I totally get it. I understand. No one knows that you're the father, and if you'd rather, I'm willing to agree to never tell anyone. I'll put 'unknown' on the birth certificate and leave it at that."

What the hell! Was she out of her mind?

The woman needed him. He had responsibilities, too. And…she had a stalker.

He stood without forethought. Then dropped to a knee in front of her. "I want my name on that certificate and everywhere else," he told her quite clearly. "I want to be totally involved every step of the way. And the only way to make this happen is for us to get married. It'll be for the baby's sake, which is the only way either one of us would ever get married—to protect the life of another—but we can make it work, Emily. As determined as we both are, we understand each other, respect each other..."

She wasn't saying anything. And he couldn't stop talking because when he did, he knew his brain was going to kick in, reminding him that he couldn't have a close one-on-one relationship with another adult. The afternoon's lesson to himself hadn't been an accident of timing.

"The marriage would have boundaries that protect us both," he continued, flying without a parachute. "It would be a non-platonic, friends-with-benefits thing, but between roommates, not soul mates."

Yeah. Roommates who shared a bedroom. Not soul mates.

"We'd have each other's backs where the kid is concerned," he added. "It'll be like working a case together again, but one that lasts a lifetime."

The tension in the invisible band squeezing his lungs lessened. Air got through. Made it to his brain.

And with rational thought taking control of the panic, he still saw his proposal as the best choice. The right choice.

Professionals working a permanent case together.

He just needed Emily to come out of her seeming state of shock and agree to marry him.

Chapter 13

Yes! They could do it. They were two peas in a pod. Professionals. They could join together in a permanent, lifelong business venture. Equal partners.

Cormac was no longer on his knee at her chair. He was pacing the end of the dining table. Back and forth. Watching her.

The intensity in his gaze lit her up.

And…

Yes! The way he'd taken for granted that they'd share a bed—a non-platonic partnership, or some such…

Her belly fluttered with the hot syrupy want he'd created within her the first time he'd kissed her.

He knew she still wanted him. How humiliating. Embarrassing.

So not cool.

But…wait.

Watching him, her gaze narrowed as she realized something else. Now she knew he still wanted her, too!

The instant thrill that shot through her gave her goose bumps. And set her insides on fire.

Until her gaze caught a corner of the pamphlet she'd shoved into her satchel.

She was going to be a mother.

She couldn't live a secret, reckless life that no one knew about.

What in the hell was this man's power over her? How did he do that to her just by standing there? Making her feel like that gorgeously hot gaze of his was actually touching her skin?

Did he know?

Did he have that effect on all the women he had sex with?

"I was looking for some motherhood groups online this afternoon," she blurted suddenly. She was grasping and not sure what she'd come up with, but it wasn't sex so she kept talking.

His perplexed-looking frown, the brief shake of his head, had her rushing forward before he could waylay her. "Pretty much all the mothers my age, or groups for mothers my age, were raising teenagers. High schoolers and college students."

He raised a hand, palm up, took a breath.

"And…and…the groups for mothers of babies," she rushed on, "a few of those mothers were twenty years younger than me."

"Emily."

"And when you look up groups for first-time mothers on social media platforms…even a lot of them are at least a decade younger," she plowed on, not at all sure where she was going, but knowing it had to be away from where he wanted them to be.

"When I take this baby to preschool, or…or…swimming lessons, or to watch… I don't know, sports or something, I might even be mistaken for a grandma. A young one, sort of, but if you do the math, not so much…"

Cormac took a step closer and she warded him off with words. "I mean, if I'd gotten married when I graduated from college and started my family, I'd be the mother of a child old enough to be graduated from college and having a baby…"

He was right in front of her, his eyes open and filled with emotion. "And…and…in birthing classes…think about that… I'm going to be one of the older ones there, too, except maybe the teacher. And that's only if I'm lucky enough to find a class with an older teacher…"

His lips covered hers. Absorbing the rest of the words racing to get out of her. Stopping all thought. Heat rushed through her. Want and need and joy.

Her mouth moved naturally, knowing how to answer him move for move, to please him, to drive him.

He moaned, fell to one knee again.

And, abruptly stood up. His mouth, his tongue, just… gone.

"See how it works?" he said then, his breathing mostly normal as he rested his hands on the back of the chair he'd been sitting in earlier, one foot crossed casually over the other.

Was he playing on her desire for him? Taunting her?

Confused, horrified, Emily shook her head, ready to get up and stumble out of the room, get her things and get out.

"You aren't in this alone, Em." He used the name he'd

greeted her with in the shower every morning they'd woken up together. "Between the two of us, we'll deal with what comes. You panic, I panic, we redirect each other, we figure it out."

Staring at him, she couldn't find any rational thoughts for a few seconds.

The kiss...wow. And, okay, he'd definitely put an end to the panic parade.

For the moment.

Because the things that scared her, worried her, even the parts of being pregnant that were elating her—they were all real. There. Between them.

They had to deal with them. As adults.

Not be distracted like a couple of kids.

She had to be the wiser one here. She had more years of life experience.

"Now, let's talk about the mothers' groups and the birthing classes," he said, throwing her off again.

What about the distraction? The—

"First, from what I've read, more women than ever are choosing to wait to have their babies in their early forties. With advances in medical science, it's safer to do so."

She hadn't read that. But she'd heard the sentiments before.

"With that in mind, I'm guessing that if you looked around you, you'd see a lot of women having babies at forty. Maybe you don't know them, or associate with them, but they're there..."

Yeah. Maybe. She'd have gotten there. If he hadn't walked in when he had.

"And the sports functions...are you really going to base your future happiness, or lack thereof, on the opinions of others? What do you care if some person is so petty, if their own life is so lacking, that they have to sit on a bleacher and judge you?"

Right. Okay, she didn't. But not everyone would be that way. Some would just glance over and naturally assume she was a grandmother...

Maybe.

And...why did she care?

"You've never cared about people's opinions on your choice to never marry..."

She'd heard a few, though. Had fielded questions about it.

But... "I consciously made that choice."

His expression changed. Went from encouraging to mostly blank. He sat.

"Look, this is a shock. I get it. Believe me, I get it. But getting married...it makes sense."

"You're serious."

"Dead serious."

Not the best choice of words.

Most particularly when she was sitting in his apartment as a way to keep from possibly being dead.

But he seemed to really want to marry her. Given the circumstances, yes, of course, but there was no changing those circumstances. They were in the dealing-with-them stage.

And marrying him...oh, God...she wanted to. For the reasons he said. It made sense. Logical sense. They'd been great together on the case they'd shared. Had solved it more quickly for working together. Their styles, their thought processes, had gelled.

And in bed...no question there.

Bed.

Bed rest. She'd had a big lump of fear in her chest

ever since Dr. Morrison had mentioned that sometimes women who gave birth over forty were more prone to having to spend the last weeks of pregnancy in a horizontal position. Who'd be there to help her with the everyday little things she wouldn't be able to do for herself? Like... like...checking the mail. Putting away the groceries?

Oh, God again, who was going to cook or go to the door to get the take-out?

Her mother would fly up, of course.

The thought didn't sit well. She'd never been the kid who could stand being taken care of by a parent.

She was way too independent for that.

But the baby's father...he owed the child, too...

She had to accept his proposal.

Stunned, Emily stared at her computer screen.

And she realized she was letting fear control her. Letting emotions make her choices, rather than maintaining the hard-won control she had over her own life.

They'd been so good together in the past for one major reason. There'd been no future ahead of them.

She'd just about made a huge mistake. One she'd made before and had promised herself, never again.

"I can't marry you, Cormac. I wouldn't be good at it, and I can't bear the thought of hurting you." The words didn't come easily, most particularly through the constrictions in her throat—the result of unshed tears. Just two months before, he'd expressed an equal abhorrence of himself in a lasting relationship. Said he'd learned the hard way. She'd related to the sentiment.

And to the fact that they hadn't had to share details. Muddy waters. They'd just gone to bed and had mind-blowing sex.

So, there they were.

As he sat still, studying her, she said what she'd known from the beginning, what she should have stuck to. "I have to go back to my place. I'll be careful. I'll keep the police escort and follow all protocol to the letter, but I have to go."

Standing, she closed the lid on her laptop, picked it up and headed down the hall.

Before she gave in to the temptation to lean over and kiss him goodbye.

Before he saw her tears.

Cormac had to let her go. Just the strength of the emotions that had been attacking him in the past couple of days was reason enough. That hadn't changed in the two months they'd been apart. And it had been the whole reason he'd gotten himself away from her the first time.

He couldn't have her relying on him when he was blinded by emotion.

But… "Emily?" he called just before she reached the spare room door.

"Yeah?" She stopped. Didn't turn around.

"It's dark outside. Can you at least wait until morning?"

She turned enough to glance his way. Her face was shadowed, but he thought she smiled a little as she nodded. "Of course."

It wasn't until after she'd shut her door that he realized they still hadn't discussed the one thing he needed to have out with her—how his role of father was going to play out.

He thought about knocking on that closed bedroom door. About getting all the tough stuff done at once, so when she went home in the morning, they'd have an understanding of how things were going to work.

He wanted to be at all future doctor appointments, for

one. How could he know where and how to step up if he wasn't even aware of the floor plan?

The blood pressure cuff…he almost knocked on the door to tell her he'd have it sent to her place as soon as it arrived the next day.

He went to bed instead. Turned his back on his own closed door and went to sleep.

And he left a note for her on the table early the next morning, telling her he'd have the cuff sent over, on his way out for an early breakfast meeting with his siblings.

He'd remain focused on what he did do well.

Work.

He was thankful that he had a talent, and a way to use it that required all of him.

Sean, Liam and Cormac had all ordered big breakfasts by the time Eva arrived to their 7 a.m. meeting. Asking for a bowl of oatmeal before she even had her coat off, she apologized for being late.

All of two minutes.

Cormac thought about giving her a hard time anyway. She'd said she needed to toughen up.

But as it occurred to him that her being the youngest, a girl, with three protective older brothers couldn't be easy, he kept his mouth shut. Why he was suddenly seeing things from her possible perspective he had no idea.

But he had no time to think about it, either, as Sean started in, letting them know that with further follow-up, there'd been absolutely no other sign, no witness, no surveillance camera proof that Humphrey had been on Amsterdam Avenue, or at Columbia the day before.

"A guy doesn't just vanish into thin air," Eva announced, sounding frustrated.

"No, but there are a lot of ways to make it appear that

he has." Cormac could come up with any number of them. Most of them unpalatable. For all they knew, Humphrey could be at the bottom of the river.

They just had to find the trail that got him there. Or wherever else he might have ended up.

Humphrey hadn't vanished. He was either removed, or he had removed himself. The removal had to be their focus.

At least until they had more to go on.

The removal. How? Why? Where to?

Had Emily left already? Removed her things from his apartment?

"I don't believe Humphrey's dead." Liam's words didn't come with their usual bravado. It was his twin's subdued tone, more than anything, that immediately grabbed Cormac's attention back from what was starting to blind him.

"I...uh...have kind of a confession to make," Liam continued, and Cormac stared. A confession?

Had Liam slipped back to his old criminal ways? And he hadn't known?

How could he not have known?

Except that...he loved his twin and—

"I've...kind of been seeing Humphrey." Liam's words slammed Cormac's mind shut.

Staring at his twin, he asked, "What do you mean, seeing him? Since he disappeared?"

The shake of Liam's head didn't ease his tension any. "Seeing him, as in, the past few years, as regularly as...a...um...patient...would."

Oh. He watched his twin. Didn't really know what else to do. Was half aware that his siblings' gazes were also trained on his twin.

"You're one of Humphrey's patients?" he asked, just to

clarify. Talk about love blinding you to what was going on right in front of your face.

He'd known Liam had struggled, of course. He'd been there with his twin through thick and thin. Even when that meant visiting him in prison. He'd just never known Liam had sought counseling...

For a few years?

He wasn't upset by the idea of his brother getting help. To the contrary, he was pretty thrilled with that part. But the fact that he hadn't known?

Mattered not at all, he realized, as his twin continued talking. "I know him, in some ways better, but definitely differently, than the rest of you, and, in my gut, I just know he's alive."

Cormac intercepted the sympathy, the compassion, in Sean's gaze as his eldest brother focused on younger twin. "It's hard on all of us, Liam. I—"

"No." Liam interrupted Sean, to look, first at him, and then at Cormac and Eva respectively. "I'm telling you, I can't explain it, but I believe, completely believe, that he's alive."

Cormac didn't know what he believed anymore. He almost blurted out that anything was possible because... guess who was going to be a father.

But the news wasn't his alone to share.

Nor was their team breakfast meeting the time to share it.

"We need to talk to Ciara again," Cormac said, getting himself firmly back on track. "To spend more time in Humphrey's home. Get a sense of what's there underneath the obvious. I mean, come on, she's, what, twenty years younger than him, knows him no time at all, and their marriage was about as whirlwind as it gets. She definitely appeared more worried than guilty, but maybe there was some connection that they were all missing.

Feeling that he was on the right track, he didn't even get a chance to hear his siblings respond, or discuss the matter further with them, before his phone blared so loudly the diners around them stared.

The new ringtone he'd set for Emily before he'd left his apartment that morning.

He might want to rethink that one. Grabbing his phone to shut it up, he glanced down and saw the text that had just hit.

911

Chapter 14

Emily was still shaking when Cormac's call came just seconds after she'd had delivery confirmation on the text she'd sent him.

"Where are you?" he asked as soon as she answered.

"Still at your apartment."

"Is someone in there?"

"No. I'm fine." She took a deep breath. "I'm sorry. I shouldn't have 911'd you. I just…"

"What's wrong?"

"I just got a call from my doorman. He said someone left a big package for me. A baby cradle, going by the box…" Her hiccup, a desperate suck of air, cut off her words.

"I'm on my way."

"Cormac?" She had to get the rest out, was thinking about the police car down below, outside his building. Hoping that whoever was in it was fully alert. She was afraid to move from the corner, her back to the wall in his dining room. She had to be able to see the room...

"Yeah?"

"There was a card with it. I had him open it." She had to get the facts out. Get a hold of herself. "It said, 'Can't wait to rock our baby in here. Watching you, dear girl. You better not be cheating on me with the PI." Her voice broke on the last bit, and she started to shake anew.

"Did you have him give the package to the police watch outside?"

"I told him to hold on to it, just until I called you," she said. "I texted the second I hung up from him."

And hadn't moved from the corner she'd crowded into while the doorman read the card. She was sitting there hunched in a ball like some kind of hunted animal.

She was shielding her baby. Cormac's phone went silent. She'd thought she lost him. She glanced at her screen to see they were still connected and was sick to her stomach.

What if Maxwell had already gotten to him?

"Just stay put," Cormac said then, as though he'd been there for those long few seconds. "I'm on my way. Stay with me on the phone until I get there."

"But..."

"Sean's on his way to your place. He'll handle the package and getting a search of the neighborhood for anyone who saw Maxwell. He's also checking on the patrol on Maxwell himself."

"You've already spoken with Sean?" She must have been on hold, not disconnected as she'd first thought.

"I was at breakfast with all three of my siblings," he said, sounding like he was running. "We came outside when I got your 911. I had you on speaker phone until we knew what was going on."

Another horror struck, giving her hot flashes. Followed by cold chills.

It was all escalating. Her world imploding.

The cradle. "Our baby."

Her doorman knew she was pregnant. And the Coltons knew? How Maxwell found out she had no idea, but the fact must have driven him over the edge. He'd lost his family and she was starting one.

And once he knew that Cormac was the father?

Cheating on me.

The man was deranged to think her being with someone would be cheating.

It made a sick kind of sense.

Somehow Maxwell was having them watched. Was there some kind of camera on her that very minute?

She ducked lower, so the dining table blocked most of the view of her from the room, feeling a bit melodramatic and lacking, but doing it anyway. "How far away are you?" she asked.

The Coltons knew.

"Ten minutes, max. Cab's pulling up. Sean just called the watch outside my apartment, and just signaled to me that there's an officer in the hall outside my door, too."

Thank God for the Coltons.

Except for...

The one thing that kept smacking her right in the face. The one thing she needed to be the least focused on right now.

"Your siblings know I'm pregnant."

"They do now."

Oh God. Oh God. Oh God.

"They don't know I'm the father."

Oh. Deep breath.

She could do it. She could be pregnant. No shame in that. Embarrassment, maybe. At her age. And not in a relationship.

Could still have been planned.

Single women had families these days.

Artificial insemination. Anonymous donor sperm.

Who cared about embarrassment or shame?

She was being stalked by a sick demented man who was going to make her pay for not putting away his cousin's killer.

He knew where she lived.

Even knew she'd stopped for a few seconds in front of a baby store the day before.

And knew who'd been with her...

"Be careful," she told Cormac. If he got shot because of her...

"Always."

"I'm serious," she said then, straightening enough against the wall to get the kink out of her back. "Watch your back."

"Again, always."

If he thought he was going to blow her off...humor her...

"Cormac. He's watching. He knew you were with me yesterday. He knows who you are, knows that you're a PI."

"I'm fully aware of that, as are my brothers and sister. And I always watch my back, Emily. It's the best way to do my job with a hope of staying alive."

Okay, then.

Right.

Only, she was shaking again.

How could it just be hitting her that her baby's father worked a very dangerous job?

One that meant he could be killed at any moment.

Fear struck her heart anew. Tightening her throat.

She didn't want Cormac to get hurt.

Didn't want her baby to grow up not knowing him.

Not just because children deserved to know their fathers. But because her baby deserved to know Cormac.

The thought was an eye-opener.

Only problem was, in her current state, she wasn't certain what she was supposed to be seeing with it.

Or what to do because of it.

When the cab Cormac was in got stuck in traffic five minutes from his building, he told Emily to hang on, threw cash at the driver, jumped out and ran. He had to get to her.

He had to know for himself that she was okay. And to be there to stand in front of her if any bullets came flying.

Or, preferably, to prevent all bullets. To find a way to get Maxwell off the streets before tragedy occurred.

"Are you running?"

"Yeah."

"Then hang up. I'll be fine."

He didn't hang up, but she did. And he upped his pace, fear for her pushing at his back.

Maxwell was smart, he'd give him that. Finding a way to continue to torment Emily without leaving a trace of evidence. An ex-accountant with one account to settle.

His own.

But he'd made a mistake, handing Cormac that cradle as evidence. The break in the case. Maxwell would have to have purchased it somewhere, with some kind of currency.

There were lots of opportunities for tracing that one. Way more than the generic bodega flowers that could be picked up most anywhere in the city without much notice.

If he got lucky, Sean would find someone who saw the ex-con deliver the cradle. Even better, there'd be surveillance camera footage of Maxwell to hang him out to dry.

Thoughts flew along with his feet, and, only slightly out of breath, he texted Emily as he rode the elevator up to his floor, letting her know his key would be sounding in the lock in seconds.

His phone rang almost immediately.

"Cormac?" Emily sounded less out of her mind with fright. Not normal, but closer to it.

"Yeah."

"I just wanted to make certain no one stole your phone or something, got your keys…"

She'd been sitting there imagining Maxwell getting to him? Winning the battle that had ensued, and managing to get by cops into his apartment to finish her off, too?

"I'm fine. And just outside the door," he said, nodding to the officer waiting as the elevator opened, to check whoever got off.

He flashed his ID.

He silently acknowledged that Emily's thoughts hadn't been that far off from his. Except that he'd been specifically trying to not think about all that could go wrong at his building before he got there. Expelling tension as he ran.

She was pacing the hallway as he came in. She stopped as soon as she saw him.

And just stood there, holding his gaze.

He wanted to go to her. To check her over, which was ludicrous; he could see she was just fine.

"Watching us at the baby store," she said, wringing her hands. "Telling me I better not be unfaithful…it's… gross. Makes me feel violated…"

"Which is his goal, Em. Don't let him succeed."

Speak to the facts, not the emotion. His role became clear. Just like that, he knew what she needed from him.

"If he could have you, he would. We're thwarting him, he knows it, so he's doing what he can to get at you in another way. If he can't have you physically, he'll try to take possession of your mind. To manipulate and control your thoughts."

She was at her seat at the table before he'd finished talking. Still looking at him. But there. "Thank you." Her gaze said so much more.

He chose to mostly not translate any of those messages.

And then he saw her bag packed and by the door.

"If you're leaving, I'm going with you," he said, without even a second to consider his words. To temper them. He'd die to save her.

End of story.

"I'm sorry if that's an imposition on your independence, or seeming as though I'm impinging on your rights, but until we get this guy, I'm sticking to you like glue. Until now he's managed to succeed in not leaving behind any actionable evidence. I'm hoping that's changed as of this morning, but he's escalating. The protection we have in place is good. So far it's kept him from you. But as he gets more desperate, so will his attempts. We can't take a chance on underestimating him."

She hadn't said a word. Or even looked like she had a word to say, which was why he'd kept on talking.

Preventing her from opening that lovely, though tense, mouth and attempting to tell him she still wanted to go home.

He ran out of words. Her silence continued.

"I can protect you better here," he said, offering one last piece of information.

When she stood, walked over to the door and took a hold of the handle on her bag, Cormac did a quick check for anything he might be able to grab to bring with him, but reached for his phone, instead, to let the protection teams know that they would be on the move.

He didn't get a single number dialed. Rather, he stood there and watched while, still without saying a word, Emily took her bag back down the hallway and into her room.

The spare room.

Her room.

He'd asked her to marry him.

She'd said no.

But what in the hell did it matter what he called the damned room?

She was staying.

Chapter 15

Being with Cormac was hard. But while they had a madman stalking them to get revenge, she felt safer with him. And since he was the professional on investigative and safety matters, doing things his way made the most sense.

And…as people passing in the night, they were in sync, as he'd just once again proven by knowing exactly what to say to calm the panic she'd allowed Maxwell's actions to raise in her, and bring her back to her sense of self.

He understood who she was.

Someone just like him in many ways.

There was emotional safety in that.

With a quick wash of her face, she put her makeup back on for a second time that morning and ran a brush through her hair. She smoothed the black velvety sweater down her thighs, over the tight black-and-white-print pants beneath them, and went out to start her day of work.

She had case files to comb through, murders with only circumstantial evidence that had resulted in convictions. She was looking for any loophole she could use to get Westmore put away for life in the event that investigators found no other provable evidence to bring her. She wasn't giving up on Josie Deveraux's return. She just couldn't afford to wait around for it, either.

Cormac, in black jeans and a white long-sleeved thermal shirt, sat across from her computer, his own laptop open. The gray sweater he'd had on when he'd come in was hanging over the top of the chair at the end of the table.

He was keeping the apartment warmer for her. He hadn't said he was. She hadn't mentioned being cold. That week.

That situation had been discussed and accounted for back in early December.

Right about the time they'd made the baby she carried.

She didn't like to walk around naked when she was freezing.

"The package was left by a courier," her PI said as she sat down across from him. Had she been there alone, she'd have been drinking some caffeine-free tea. Doing so with him there seemed a little too cozy—too much like cohabitation. "He said some guy in a dark coat, with a scarf and hood, paid him a hundred bucks to deliver the box to your building."

Maxwell.

"Seeing me looking at the baby stuff…do you think it unhinged him?" She asked what she'd been wondering while she waited for Cormac to get home.

"I'm hoping so. The quicker he escalates, the faster we'll catch him. Buying that cradle was a mistake. There

Loyal Readers
FREE BOOKS Voucher

We're giving away

THOUSANDS of **FREE BOOKS**

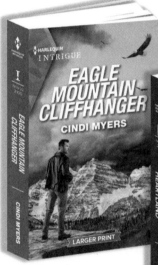

Don't Miss Out! Send for Your Free Books Today!

See Details Inside

Get up to 4
FREE FABULOUS BOOKS
You Love!

To thank you for being a loyal reader we'd like to send you up to 4 FREE BOOKS, absolutely free when you try the Harlequin Reader Service.

Just write "YES" on the Loyal Reader Voucher and we'll send you 2 free books from each series you choose and Free Mystery Gifts, altogether worth over $20.

Try **Harlequin® Romantic Suspense** books featuring heart-racing page-turners with unexpected plot twists and irresistible chemistry that will keep you guessing to the very end.

Try **Harlequin Intrigue® Larger-Print** books featuring action-packed stories that will keep you on the edge of your seat. Solve the crime and deliver justice at all costs.

Or **TRY BOTH** and get 2 books from each series!

Your free books are completely free, even the shipping! If you continue with your subscription, you can look forward to curated monthly shipments of brand-new books from your selected series, always at a discount off the cover price! Plus you can cancel any time.

So don't miss out, return your Loyal Readers Voucher today to get your Free books.

Pam Powers

LOYAL READER
FREE BOOKS VOUCHER

YES! I Love Reading, please send me up to 4 FREE BOOKS and Free Mystery Gifts from the series I select.

Just write in "YES" on the dotted line below then return this card today and we'll send your free books & gifts asap!

➡ YES ⬅
- - -

Which do you prefer?

☐ **Harlequin® Romantic Suspense**
240/340 HDL GRS9

☐ **Harlequin Intrigue® Larger-Print**
199/399 HDL GRS9

☐ **BOTH**
240/340 & 199/399
HDL GRTL

FIRST NAME _____ LAST NAME _____

ADDRESS _____

APT.# _____ CITY _____

STATE/PROV. _____ ZIP/POSTAL CODE _____

EMAIL ☐ Please check this box if you would like to receive newsletters and promotional emails from Harlequin Enterprises ULC and its affiliates. You can unsubscribe anytime.

HI/HRS-622-LR_LRV22

are only so many places you can get them in the city. Sean already has people canvassing them all."

"Unless he bought it online. Overnight delivery. And paid for it with a generic gift card. They're easy enough to come by…"

"We've got someone checking delivery services," he told her.

"He could have had it dropped somewhere else, so we can't trace it to him."

"Like whatever apartment he's cleaning today," Cormac said, and made another call to his older brother.

"He's under surveillance. Someone had to have seen him carrying the box. It's not like he could hide that under his hood," she heard him say. And then, right afterward… "Unless he hid it in his trash bin as he was leaving…he pushes a cart in and out of every job. Find out where he dumps that bin after a job. Maybe there are cameras there."

He nodded. Hung up.

"Sean doesn't get uptight when you give him orders?"

"I was actually talking to Liam. He's with Sean and picked up. But no. We each have our strengths and trust each other enough to work together to get the job done."

For a second there, she was…envious.

She'd never had siblings. Or any family other than her parents. And since they'd retired to Florida, she spent most holidays and birthdays either with friends or alone.

It didn't sound as if Cormac was ever alone for major moments, unless he specifically chose to be.

Major moments.

A baby coming into the Colton family was going to be huge.

And that child…would never be alone.

The baby growing inside her was being born into a legacy of love and loyalty.

"What?" he asked, and she realized he'd been watching her. His brow creased in concern, he asked, "Are you feeling sick?"

"Of course not. I'm as healthy as a horse. I just…your family… I guess we need to talk about you telling them about the baby." It was only right.

"The only people in my life who are going to care that I've kept the secret from them are my parents," she continued, "and they'll understand completely. No sense in getting their hopes up until I'm far enough along to pretty much ensure a live birth. Your siblings…they know I'm pregnant…they're going to be hurt that you withheld the part about you being the father."

With a sideways tilt of his head, he said, "I wouldn't go that far. Pissed maybe, yeah."

"They might see it as a breach of that trust you just mentioned."

"So, what, you've been insisting I say nothing, but now you think I'm wrong not to tell them." His look pierced her.

God, life was complicated.

Which was precisely why she'd chosen to live it alone.

"I'm saying that I'm seeing things from a perspective other than my own, which I should have been doing all along, and that while it's not detrimental to my relationships to withhold the information at this point, I think it could reflect negatively on yours."

"You want me to tell them."

What, was he basing it all on her permission? That didn't feel good, either.

"No, I don't *want* you to tell them. But I think you *should*."

"Just disregard your feelings, you're saying."

With a shrug, she studied him, needing answers she couldn't find. "This is why I don't do relationships," she muttered, and went back to work.

Emily's stalker was a ghost. He came and went without being noticed—a feat that was not as hard as it might seem, considering the millions of people crowding New York streets, coming and going with heads down to ward off the chill, and all bundled up in coats and hoods and scarves.

What was one more coat, hood and scarf among them?

Either that, or Maxwell was diabolically smart, and Cormac wasn't going to concede that point. Diabolically angry, yes. He'd give Maxwell that one.

None of the stores in the city that carried the make and model of cradle left for Emily recognized Maxwell's picture. They were waiting on warrants to go through the receipts for those that were purchased, in order to compare the list against Emily's databases and lists.

No one remembered seeing a man carrying a cradle—which pointed again to Maxwell's cleaning cart as the perfect hiding place.

And that would also explain why the police details watching him hadn't noticed him coming and going with the package. The courier couldn't remember the exact corner that he'd taken the package. The guy had just called out to him while he was on his way someplace else. Someplace that was enough in the vicinity of an apartment Maxwell had been assigned to clean early that morning to have pointed to him. It wasn't like he was being followed inside buildings. He could have slipped out a side door. Found the closest courier riding by. Made his transaction and taken his cleaning cart back inside.

Still, someone had to have delivered the cradle to a place Maxwell could pick it up, the most obvious being the building in which he'd been cleaning. Sean was getting warrants for shipping records.

A handwriting analysis showed that both cards had been written by the same person. Most likely male.

It was telling that he'd written on the cards himself, rather than generating them through a computer. It was one more sign that the moves against Emily were personal.

Nothing got more personal than revenge.

They were stuck working from inside his apartment because there was no way in hell he was taking Emily out when they had no idea how Maxwell had seen them outside the baby shop the day before. Cormac was going back over the list Emily had made based on recent convict releases related to her cases.

He was checking first to see if any of them had been in the same prison as Maxwell. Which, considering that there were only so many prisons to send them to, was a yes. He then started in on cellblocks. Tedious work, but that's what PIs did, spending the time to examine every spot of dust, just in case.

It made more sense that Maxwell could pull off his payback without being noticed if he had help. Someone they weren't looking for. Or asking about.

After a salad lunch, Emily had gone to her room to make some calls regarding the Brinkley murder. It made him nervous, having her out of sight. But he welcomed the respite from her compelling company just the same.

He didn't think as straight when Emily Hernandez was in the same room as him. Something he'd realized about a week into their relationship in December.

And was the sole reason he'd split immediately upon making the discovery.

It was some kind of sick irony, his baby growing inside her. No way he was ever going to escape her completely. Not even when he died.

That baby was going to hold them together forever.

Just the thought filled him with enough angst to run ten miles. Hard.

By the time Emily came back out, sometime midafternoon, he'd done as much cross-checking of the names on her list as he could and had started in on individuals again. Checking social media pages, contacts, posts. Not only of those named but also following trails of any friends and associates he found, too.

He was looking for anything that led him back to Maxwell.

Or anything that could tie another perp to the attacks against Emily. He knew he had his guy, but Cormac was Cormac. He didn't leave stones unturned.

You risked getting blindsided when you did that.

His life was definitely testimony to that one.

Emily was in the kitchen making tea.

"You want some?" she asked, standing there in the long sweater and long, leg-hugging black-and-white pants. Like they were begging a guy to notice what was beneath them.

Hell, yes, he wanted some.

He shook his head. Went back to studying the various screens he had up on his computer.

He was going to have a child. A boy or a girl? Named after his father? Maybe with Kelly as a middle name?

What the hell.

Again.

A new email popped up, and Cormac clicked, leaning forward to jump on the lifeboat that had just presented itself.

Sean had sent him a scanned copy of the note left with the cradle. And various close-ups of the box.

He opened all the photos together on his screen. The roses. The note that came with them. The cradle. And that card. He needed them to tell him something. The vernacular. The handwriting. To show him something about the man behind them that would lead him somewhere. Give him something they could use to nail the fiend.

Emily sat across from him. Even the look of concentration on her face as she worked was a turn-on.

If she'd gone home, he could have lost her. Instead of delivering a cradle, Maxwell, who was watching them somehow, would be working on a way to grab her.

A janitor in an apartment building, disguised as a woman…or someone heavier than Maxwell. Anything to get by without being recognized.

Grabbing his phone, he sent a text to the immediate protection crew, which also included Sean, to have everyone check any cleaning crew in his building.

To check anyone coming and going who didn't live in the building.

He heard back, almost immediately, that there was no janitorial service in his building that day. And that they'd post someone in the lobby, checking every delivery person who entered for the next day, at least.

An ADA being threatened to that extent put the whole justice system at risk.

When he told Emily about the extra detail that had been assigned to her case, she looked up at him, nodded, but went right back to work.

He got it.

Putting work first was how they lived.

Except...they had a baby coming.

And like it or not, that was a game changer.

He just had no idea how to play the new game.

Chapter 16

With her life flying so high out of her control she wasn't sure she'd ever be able to grab hold again, Emily put herself in a mental time-out. Any thoughts that popped up with stressful emotion attached were immediately rejected. She took her focus on a deep dive into any cases she sat on as first chair, searching for links to Humphrey Kelly.

When that turned up nothing, she searched the case database for any that had his name associated, looking for anything that might be familiar to her. Maybe a defendant had associated the two of them together, even if she didn't.

She ended up with a decent list of names on that one. And she recognized most of them because she'd been consulted on a few of Kelly's cases, privately in the office. Mostly it was just brainstorming stuff. Nothing a defendant would know.

Still, she looked for the verdict on each case. Crossed off all that were listed as not guilty. Then she ran a comparison between her list and their earlier retrieved list of recent prison releases.

That gave her one name. Blake Nygren.

The man was already on her original list because she'd put him away for assault with a deadly weapon. It was a name still on their list because the man had given her the creeps with his intimidating stares in the courtroom.

"Hey," she said, looking up at the man she'd been trying to pretend was just one of her work associates. His dark hair askew, as though he'd been running his hand over it, Cormac looked…tired.

This was an expression she didn't recognize on him. The man had always seemed vibrant even sound asleep.

When tenderness welled up inside her, she clamped down and said, "I've found another case that ties Humphrey and me together. I mean, not really, but from the defendant's perspective…"

Out of his seat immediately, Cormac came around the table and looked over her shoulder at her screen.

"Blake Nygren," he read aloud from the case file she'd pulled up. "Humphrey testified on behalf of a female prison guard who claimed Nygren had come on to her, and then had threatened her when she said she was going to report him. Nygren said she was the one who'd come on to him. He had people, fellow prisoners and another guard, who testified on his behalf. The guard dropped the case but asked for a transfer."

"Yeah, and look at this," she said, bringing up another screen. "Nygren has a couple of domestic violence calls on his record, dating back twenty years ago, both dropped when his girlfriend refused to testify. I couldn't use them in court and had forgotten about them, but a judge was allowing them in for this most recent one."

Looking at the ex-con's earlier booking photo, she shivered. She glanced up at Cormac for distraction from the panic that started to settle in her belly again.

His gaze held hers. A second. Two. Then, turning his head, he pulled his phone out of his pocket. "He was with his parole officer yesterday. I'll check in."

But she heard him make a call to his brother first. Asking Sean to get someone on Nygren immediately, to bring him in for questioning regarding Humphrey Kelly's disappearance.

It was a good move. Tie him to the one—you had more chance to get him for the other.

Cormac left the room as he talked to his brother. She could hear his muffled voice coming from down the hall. Then silence.

Followed by a toilet flushing.

And the intimacy of their situation hit her all over again. Filling her face with heat that slid down to other regions.

She was pregnant with his child. A little late to worry about awareness of naked parts and body functions.

And she couldn't just walk away and go home. Not if she wanted to live long enough to birth the baby growing inside her.

And she did want that.

More than she'd ever wanted anything else in her life.

When Cormac came back out to the dining room, Emily had the Brinkley murder file open on the table beside her computer.

"The Nygren thing, just made me wonder if maybe

there's something attached to Westmore or Lana Brinkley, something from the past that might have something to do with Humphrey Kelley," she said. "Since that's my current case, and, as you've said, Humphrey went missing such a short time before someone tried to grab me and both instances happened in the area of the courthouse."

"Find anything?" he asked, and then, after she shook her head, sat back down with an eye to…he didn't know what.

Getting the woman to say she'd marry him.

So they could get on with it all.

Including having sex again.

They were playing a dangerous game—thinking they could avoid the obvious. The way they kept getting caught up looking at each other, the verdict was already in.

They might as well get on with the sentencing.

If nothing else, it would release some of the tension trying to strangle them. From his point of view, at least.

Yeah, like that. She'd looked over at him. Her lips hadn't moved, but those eyes were giving him more than he could decipher in mere words.

A woman didn't look at a guy like that unless she was either the best actress ever, or she had it for him. Bad.

Trouble was, he couldn't be sure what his gaze was saying back to her. Wasn't sure he was ready to know.

And wasn't sure he could stand by whatever nonverbal promise he might be making.

He wanted her to believe that she was safe because he'd protect her. And he would. With his life if need be, but guaranteeing he'd be successful…

Couldn't do it.

He wanted her to know that they could resume their incredible sex life without things getting too messy.

But how did he do that when he was scared to death they couldn't?

"You ever hear of Willa Burford?" He heard the words before he'd fully registered his decision to say them. He immediately wanted to take them back.

Emily blinked. She looked offended for an instant, as though he'd insulted her somehow. But then she frowned.

"It rings a bell," she said. "Was it a case the DA's office handled?"

He shook his head. Told himself to take his last chance to let it drop.

"She was a private investigator."

Emily's suddenly flat expression nearly stopped him. Should have stopped him.

"We worked together on a couple of cases. Became lovers…"

"Stop." She stood up. "No need to do this."

"Please, sit down." He didn't command. Half hoped she'd walk out on him.

Just down the hall, to her room. He sure as hell didn't want to push her out the door.

But they had to get on with things. She was having his kid.

Avoiding the subject couldn't possibly be good parenting.

"Weeks led into months, we were monogamous, making long-term plans, like we were going to be together forever."

"And let me guess, you walked out on her, broke her heart, and now don't trust yourself not to do the same to the baby and me."

His brow shot up before he could stop it. Wow. Not at all what he was expecting.

But…interesting.

Where had it come from?

Eyes narrowing, he leaned in a bit. "Is that my story you're telling there, Hernandez, or yours?"

Chin jutted, lips pursed, she nodded. Emily crossed her arms and said, "Yeah, okay, it could be mine, but that doesn't mean I'm wrong about you. We said we were made of the same cloth."

"As it happens, you are wrong about me," he said, no longer feeling as intense a need to get his story out. "But now I want to know whose heart you broke."

He wanted to be kidding, half teasing, but wasn't. At all.

True to course, she wasn't giving up anything, either. He stared her down. Had to know.

A good investigator knew you had to follow the facts to solve a case.

"I was engaged," she said, and his breath caught for a second. Emily, engaged? When he couldn't get her to even seriously talk about a future for them?

Him, wanting a future with anyone?

As non-platonic roommates, he reminded himself. Because of the baby.

"Paul was a college professor, growing his career, just as I was. Yet, he somehow managed to eke out time for me, too. I didn't do the same. The demands on a junior prosecutor were onerous. And not just in terms of time. The drain on my emotions was huge when I first started spending my days sifting through witness statements, combing through evidence of horrendous things that had happened to good people, some just children…"

She shrugged. She was reciting facts she clearly owned. And was comfortable with. He admired that about her.

"Most nights I'd come home depleted, with nothing left to give anywhere else. Anyway, when I saw what I was doing to him, and was honest with myself, knowing that I couldn't give any less to my job, I broke things off with him. And broke his heart a bit in the process, too. He definitely left me more jaded than he'd been when he came into my life."

He got it. Completely. "Which is why I fit in so well," he said, feeling comfortable in his own skin for a second or two as well. "No one's more jaded than I am."

Assessing him, she grinned. "Maybe, but you're still so vibrant, still thinking you can change your portion of the world…"

"And you don't?" He pinned her gaze with his own. Purposely. Needing honesty between them, if nothing else.

Which was why he'd started the damned conversation to begin with.

Eventually, she shrugged again, but didn't look away. "I'd lost some of that vitality," she said then, shocking him. "Until you."

Oh, hell. He didn't know what to do with that.

"Maybe I'd gotten a little complacent in my ability to do my job successfully. And well. You, with your passion for all facets of the truth, challenged me to go deeper, look for more, again. So, thank you for that."

She smiled. A generic, though probably sincere, expression of gratitude.

He nodded. No closer to being…anywhere…than he'd been before he'd opened his mouth in forbidden territory.

But ready to get back to work.

Maybe she was right.

They were two people married to their jobs and trying to find more was wrong.

He just wasn't sure where that left the baby she was carrying.

"Uh, excuse me…" Emily had tried to not be offended when, as soon as she'd made her confessions and proclamations, Cormac had returned his attention to his computer screen.

She could have turned to her own laptop for at least partial answers. Willa Burford. The name really was familiar. She couldn't recall why but could look it up.

Chances were, with her access to court records, she could find something.

"What?" Cormac glanced over at her, but not without a few seconds' lapse, as though he was so deeply engaged in life-and-death work that she really wouldn't want to disturb him.

At the moment, Willa Burford seemed like life and death to her.

Ridiculous. But she was forty-three and pregnant and had a sicko stalker who wanted to make her pay personally for holding him accountable to his own bad choices.

Cormac could just go ahead and sue her for not being the most perfect version of herself. Or on her best behavior.

"Willa Burford?" And when he just shrugged, shook his head, she still couldn't let it go. "Turnabout's fair play, Cormac."

And even if it wasn't…

He seemed about to argue, but then, after a couple of seconds he nodded, pushed his laptop to the left, folded his hands on the table and faced her. Looking her straight in the eye, he said, "She's the reason I can't be in a committed, one-on-one long-term relationship."

"What in the hell do you think a marriage is?" Her tone wasn't calm. She couldn't help it. The man was…maddening. Pursuing her, leaving her. Asking her to marry him. Refusing to talk about anything but work.

Reach out. Abandon.

The pattern did not bode well for any future with him in it.

"Ah," he said, raising one finger, and then folding his hands back together. As though the move was a deliberate act meant to help him somehow with the conversation ahead.

Keep him calm?

Professional?

She was still waiting for whatever came after the "ah."

"The roommate part of it, that's what keeps it from being one-on-one. For people like us, it's perfect," he continued, leaning toward her until his impressively manly chest met the table. "You don't have to worry about breaking another heart with your single-focused work drive. And I…"

He, what?

Then it hit her. He'd said that his leaving a broken heart behind hadn't happened. Which meant…he'd been left with one?

It didn't seem possible. Cormac was…everything a woman…no. Not necessary to go there. She had someplace else to be. "Willa left you?"

Lips tight, he loosened them enough to lick them and stared at her. "In a manner of speaking."

She'd hurt him, all right. So badly that he wasn't going

to ever let another woman close to his heart, Emily surmised. Not even her.

The fact couldn't possibly hurt as much as she thought it did in the moment. She'd have to care for Cormac a whole lot more than she did for it to really hurt so badly she felt something crumbling inside.

It was just the drama of the past few days getting to her. Nearly being kidnapped, then being stalked. Finding out she was pregnant...

Living in protective custody inside Cormac Colton's apartment...

It all made sense, but she couldn't let it go at that. "What does that mean, exactly? In a manner of speaking?"

She'd spelled her life out clearly for him. And he needed to do the same before she could have a serious discussion with him about anyone's future.

"She didn't actually choose to leave."

"You kicked her out." Which meant, basically, they were back where they'd started. He'd broken Willa's heart, and, like Emily, had made the choice never to hurt another human being in the same way again.

"No." He tapped a thumb hard against the hand it held. "Think, Emily. Willa Burford. A private investigator..." He drew the word out.

There was something. She wasn't grasping it. But then, her mind wasn't in the best frame now.

"The Silo Cartel..."

Drugs. And...it all came back to her. A female PI, employed exclusively by the police department, had been secretly working for the cartel. When a joint task force had moved in to take down the cartel, she'd been killed.

"Willa Burford," she said aloud.

There'd been some talk that someone had set her up…

Eyes wide, she stared at Cormac. "You knew? You figured it out and…"

Sitting back, he didn't break eye contact with her as he said, "Nope. And if I hadn't been called out on another job, I might have been killed with her. Someone on the task force found out she was dirty, and for a short time there, they weren't sure if I was in on it or not. They didn't get her killed, by the way. They planned to get her out. But she knew she was made, got scared and screwed up."

"She told you she was made? That she was scared?"

Another shake of his head. "I had no idea about any of it. No idea that she was helping to put pounds of cocaine on city streets, that she was amassing a small fortune, that she'd been made, or knew she'd been made. I kissed her goodbye that morning, left to question a possible gun-runner, thinking that we really did have a future together."

He sounded disgusted with himself.

Betrayed, she could understand. Pissed at Willa, or even the world in general, sure. But disgusted?

"How can you possibly blame yourself for trusting the woman you expected to spend the rest of your life with?" She wasn't a counselor, by any means, but she had eleven years of life experience on him, and she could definitely assure him that the man he'd been was the kind most women dreamed of having and not as many were lucky enough to find.

"Trust is one thing," he said. "You trust someone until they blow your trust. Or, if you're lucky, they don't and you trust them forever. Like my siblings. I hope.

Though, for a time there, Liam was questionable..." He half grinned.

She didn't even hint at cracking a smile. Couldn't relent at that point.

Then his gaze sharpened as it poured into hers. "I'm blind when it comes to matters of the heart, Emily. I get close, I lose sight. Willa died because I was so damned blind to the trouble she'd gotten herself into, that I couldn't help her get out of it alive."

"She was a trained PI. She knew how to hide what she was doing. And had the perfect cover to do so. You can hardly blame yourself for her being as good as she was at her job."

He shook his head. "I'm a trained PI, too. One of the best. Looking back, there were signs. Things I should have seen. Things I would have seen if I hadn't been so hooked."

For a split second there, Emily was jealous of a dead traitor.

"They say love is blind," he said then, his expression implacable. "In my case, it's true."

She didn't know what to say to that. Wasn't even sure what she was thinking. Her heart was pounding, and dread filled her stomach.

And all she could come up with was, "And yet you still think we should get married."

Because, obviously, he didn't love her.

Which was fine, because she wasn't ever going to fall in love again, either. She wasn't good at it. A man's heart wasn't safe with her unless he was fine with coming in second on her list every single time. Actually, now third.

Work was going to have to take second place, at least for the next eighteen years or so.

"I'm going to need you to look out for my blind spots. The baby's going to need you watching out for the things I'm not going to see," Cormac told her.

Because he'd love his child. Maybe already did, if he was anything like her. And they'd already established that he was.

Wow.

And just like that…they'd established it.

They loved their baby.

It didn't seem possible to fall so hard in just a few days for something that wasn't even viable yet.

Didn't seem possible that she was sitting across the table from Cormac Colton sort of discussing marriage, either.

The baby's going to need you watching out for the things I'm not going to see.

His last words still rang through her head.

"And me?" she asked. "Who's going to look out for me?"

But she knew the answer to that.

She was.

"I am," Cormac said then, surprising her so much her mouth fell open. "That's why we'll be roommates, not soul mates."

And she got it. Closed her mouth.

He wasn't in love with her. Wasn't going to fall in love with her. So he wasn't blind where she was concerned. How could she expect otherwise? She was more than a decade older than he was.

That's why we'll be roommates, not soul mates.

He said the words like they were a gift.

And really, considering the person she knew herself to be, they should have been.

So, why weren't they?

Chapter 17

"Maxwell's not answering his door or his phone." Cormac broke the news to Emily just after they ordered and ate dinner.

She had cleared away the leftover dinner debris but was otherwise silent, and had been more focused than he'd seen her in a while as her gaze moved from computer screen to the legal pad on one side of her and the files on the other. It was as though their conversation—which had left him nowhere, with nothing settled, since she'd failed to accept his proposal or even indicate she was leaning that way—had somehow given her whatever answers she'd needed.

Her life was at risk. Their baby's future hung in the balance, and she was consumed by work.

She'd warned him.

Truth be told, he had been focused on work, too, until

he'd just had the text about Maxwell and looked up at her beautiful face across from him, with the knowledge that she was in extreme danger. He faced her grimly. "And because I can't seem to find one piece of concrete proof that he's behind any of these threats against you, we can't get a warrant to enter his place. We can bring him in again for questioning, but only if we get him to answer the door, and Sean isn't sure what any more questioning is going to do, except let the man know we've basically got nothing on him. He's managed to outsmart all of us at least to the extent that he's, so far, getting away with terrorizing you."

"But he hasn't gotten me," Emily said, her gaze warm as she landed on him.

"He's found a way to get past the detail watching him," he said, refusing to fall into the compelling pool of emotion that Emily seemed to invite him to. "Some disguise, maybe, I don't know yet, but I've got Sean sending me all the surveillance footage he can find from all sides of Maxwell's residence. If he's coming and going as someone else, I'll find him."

He had timetables, knew when the man was at work. When he picked up the cleaning van, when he dropped it off. Knew when he'd been seen coming and going. If another body—most likely female was his guess—was coming and going only at times when they didn't have eyes on Maxwell...

In the meantime, "Nygren's out," he told her, while he had her attention. "Sean's had a tech at the precinct spending hours scouring footage from Atlantic City, and they finally got him. He wasn't even in New York the other morning during your attempted abduction. And he was picked up last night, back in Atlantic City for assault. He was drunk off his ass."

Not a good guy. But not their stalker either.

And the list of recent prison releases from cases she'd prosecuted was dwindling. He was going over it one more time, just to cross his t's and dot his i's. Was down to just a few names.

"This Peter Bezos," he said, Willa firmly in mind as he kept himself focused on keeping Emily safe. "How sure are you that he's not a concern?"

"About as sure as I can be," she told him. "He emailed me a couple of days ago to say he'd heard about my near abduction, to offer his condolences…"

Sitting up straight, Cormac homed in on that. Perps liked to insinuate themselves into investigations. Especially ones who were mentally wrong enough to stalk an ADA. "He emailed you?"

"Yeah." She scrolled. Typed. "I just sent it to you."

How could she not be concerned? She was no rookie. She *knew* how this kind of offender had to be a part of things. "Two days ago and you're only just now telling me?"

"I didn't tell you about the other couple hundred or so emails I've received from lawyers, judges and clerks, either," she replied. "My work and my colleagues are my life and my family."

Okay, but she hadn't put any of the others away.

"I've had emails from some victims, too, and from a few others that I prosecuted who've been out with lack of recidivism. People who've written to thank me in the past, that kind of thing. Bezos is one of those. Besides, as you can see, he's reapplying for his law license," she finished.

He verified that with the post that had just come in from her.

It left him feeling like a bit of an overreactive fool. "I didn't know you could do that," he said, trying to save face, while he was pissed at himself for feeling like he needed to do so. He wasn't there to impress Emily.

Had nothing to prove.

He had a job to do, one that he excelled at, and that meant not overlooking anyone. Not assuming anything.

"In the state of New York, you wait seven years after being disbarred, and then, depending on a pretty specific set of circumstances, you can reapply. He qualifies and is doing so. He thanked me for helping him earn his second chance with my letter to his parole board."

Could he keep his distance from the woman who was pregnant with his kid and still admire the hell out of her? She didn't just care about numbers, cases won, convictions made, her career count. She cared about people. Even the ones she put in prison.

That said a hell of a lot more about her than anything else he knew.

The screen on his computer populated, drawing his attention, and everything else faded away as he read.

"What?" The sudden alarm in Emily's voice grabbed him. It mirrored his senses, which were on full alert.

"What?" he asked back, focused on her first and foremost. He had a situation—but that didn't make hers any less important.

"I was asking you what, your expression, something just happened over there…"

She'd been watching him. No time to like the fact.

"James Kinney…"

The seventy-year-old man she'd dismissed as not a

threat. She'd said she'd spoken at his parole hearing. He was mean, violent when he drank but had been dry for five years.

"What about him?" She still didn't sound concerned.

"I identified him in the crowd gathering around the courthouse about an hour after your abduction."

"He lives in the area."

"Yeah, but I've just been running a series of searches on him, as well as his family, friends, any known associates, and this isn't good."

He turned his computer around so she could see. The family of the woman he'd killed on a drunken binge thirty years before, but hadn't been prosecuted for until ten years later, had just posted that they feared for their lives. The man was out to get everyone who he claimed lied about the woman's death. And he was drinking again.

Face white, Emily looked from the computer screen up to him. "Can you verify this?"

"I just sent a screenshot to Sean," he told her.

And found it a little hard to breathe when her eyes filled with gratitude. And something more.

It was that something more that made him uneasy as hell and filled him with an intense need to take her to bed.

She had to excuse herself. Get away.

Before she did something she'd regret for the rest of her life. She could not fall for Cormac Colton. She just couldn't.

In her normal life, there wouldn't even have been the possibility. But with all the drama, her life in danger from a deranged stalker, finding out she was going to be a mother, being cooped up with the one man who'd managed to turn her crank far enough to unhinge her for a moment when he broke things off…it was getting to her.

Cormac's phone rang seconds after he'd turned his screen to her; he'd shown her the caller ID, it was Sean, and she booked.

Grabbed her computer, her files, and went down the hall to her bedroom.

Half an hour later, when she heard Cormac moving around the apartment, she texted him to say that she was turning in early.

He'd texted back immediately, asking if she felt okay.

Yes, she'd sent back and left it at that.

His concern was because of the baby, she surmised. She'd given him a long rundown on all the increased risks to her pregnancy due to her age. And he loved that unknown child. The thought broke her heart a little—broke it enough to let in the surge of good feeling that realization brought her. Her baby was going to be one very lucky, very loved child.

In an atypical family setting.

Young dad. Older mom. Not married. Not in love. Just friends.

Or married, but just non-platonic roommates?

She couldn't see it.

But if it would be best for the baby? Better than living with a single, workaholic mother, and only getting visitation with the single, workaholic father?

Really, with both her and Cormac working such long hours, typically gone so much, how hard would it be to share the same apartment?

And the baby would have one or other parent around, in the same home, with more frequency. She was always home at night. And Cormac, as she remembered it, had been home until noon some mornings. When he was using technology to ferret out information.

As he had that night.

On James Kinney.

It hadn't felt like a seventy-year-old arm squeezing her and pushing her toward the car door the other morning. But what did she know of a seventy-year-old newly released convict's physical state? If he'd worked out the nearly twenty years he'd been put away. Had worked manual labor, and needed to keep himself fit to stay alive?

She soaked in the tub for a bit, trying to relax, but instead, she was getting het up, thinking of Cormac so close, pretty sure that if she called out to him, he'd join her in the bubbles. So she ended bath time and took her computer to bed instead. Looked over the James Kinney file.

And got agitated in an entirely different way.

Giving herself a break, considering that she'd been working for more than twelve hours and she was pregnant, she switched to a streaming app, scrolled to an old sitcom she practically knew by heart, and, with the computer propped by the pillow next to her, fell asleep.

The next time she opened her eyes, the view outside the opened curtain in her room was blanketed with snow.

And activity on the street below was…nil.

Pulling up the weather app on her phone, she saw why. An overnight snowstorm had dropped more than eighteen inches of snow in the city, pretty much trapping her and Cormac together in his apartment.

When a burst of anticipation surged through her, she dropped her phone, gathered gray pants, a black sweater and underthings, took herself to the shower, and kept the water tepid. Warm enough not to make her uncomfortable, but not hot enough to feel really good.

Life was giving her challenges beyond anything she'd ever faced before. She was not going to fail herself.

Or the child that was already dependent upon her.

She was a mature woman. With a notable, successful, somewhat high-profile career. Not a youngster who could be forgiven a girlish crush.

As she reminded herself, with little patience, when she walked into the dining room, satchel over her shoulder, and computer and files in hand, to see Cormac, in flannel pants and a T-shirt, already in his seat hard at work.

"We're snowed in," he said, his glance barely grazing her before he returned his attention to the screen.

His hair looked fresh-from-the-shower combed. He hadn't shaved.

Would it be completely inappropriate to ask him to go put on some jeans?

Figuring the obvious was better left unsaid, she set her things down, plugged in her computer and went out to make tea.

If ever a day could be excruciatingly endless, Cormac figured that one trapped inside with Emily Hernandez was it. He'd known he was going to be glued to her, and that keeping her out of sight was better than not, but with no ability to leave…the job took on all new meaning.

They weren't just in protective custody; they were in a world that was literally just the two of them.

"At least we can assume this means that Maxwell can't get to me," she said, sometime around lunch, when he'd come back from the kitchen with a plate of leftover pasta. He'd offered to heat some for her, but she'd said she was going to have a salad, instead.

The baby diet and all, he figured.

He'd spent the morning weeding his way through hours of tape Sean had sent over on Eugene Maxwell. Sean was good. He'd managed to procure footage from cameras all along Maxwell's block, as well as from buildings behind and beside Cormac's.

He'd moved from the dining room table. He just couldn't continue to sit so close to Emily that he could catch whiffs of the soap she used. Or see her beautiful face every time he looked up. He hadn't been able to stay in his bedroom for long, either, as very real erotic memories of her in there with him kept surfacing. He'd changed into jeans. And his tightest pair of underwear. As punishment to the body part that refused to follow orders.

Less than an hour post lunch, after gazing out the front window to the deserted street below, watching the flakes still floating down on top of what was already a crippling amount of snow, he landed his butt on the couch.

Emily, hard at work on the Westmore case he assumed, was flashing through various screens and taking notes. He could see her laptop if he turned around.

So he quit doing that.

Amazing how two people forced into severely close proximity could say so few words in so many hours. He was grateful for their mutual dedication to their jobs. To their similar abilities to focus.

Not surprisingly, he was slowly filling with tension, too, brought on by all of the things unspoken between them. He'd asked, midmorning when she'd taken a five-minute break, how she was feeling. Had received a one word "fine" for his effort.

His offer to provide lunch had come back rejected.

And…there it was again. The purple hood, tied with a pink scarf. Midthigh-length purple coat belted at the waist, boots zipped over pants. Pink gloves.

Scrolling back and opening multiple files, he observed, checked time stamps and sat up.

Double-checked.

Opened copies of tapes he hadn't yet seen.

And sat up.

"Maxwell's using a disguise," he said aloud. Just blurted it right out there.

And turned around to see Emily sliding quickly in her chair to stare at him. Mouth open. Fear chasing across her expression. It was the first time since she'd walked out the night before that their glances had met.

The power there, the tumult of emotions—hers and his—spilled all over him.

"I have to look at the other tapes," he said, grabbing his phone to call his brother. "On the street by the baby store. Outside your place. As soon as this damned weather lets up, we can get a recanvas of bodegas and subway stops for flower purchases. If he's this far gone, is this determined to get his revenge, he's probably got a fake ID, too. Wouldn't be a stretch to assume he's got the connections to do so…"

He just kept looking into those compelling brown eyes, speaking his thoughts aloud, as though if he just kept talking, he could keep her from speaking. He could prevent her from releasing her fear and blinding him to what he had to do. He continued to hold on to her gaze as, still talking, he dialed his brother. Repeating a lot of what he'd just said, he ended with, "I need the tapes from Emily's building, too." A techie could check for the purple and pink attire, but he wanted to do it himself.

Had to do it himself. One way or another, he was going to find the evidence they needed to get Emily's stalker off the street, to free her from the debilitating fear that was robbing her of the freedom she valued so highly. That was making her look at him with a helplessness he couldn't bear.

He would not fail her.

Nor was he going to get up off the couch and take her in his arms. Not even for a second. He couldn't afford the distraction.

"We'll get him, Em," he said, schooling his voice as he had when speaking with his brother. He was all business.

Breaking eye contact with Emily, he went back to work.

Chapter 18

After emailing Cormac a copy of her finished list of all the cases Humphrey Kelly had worked on that she also had some kind of association with, Emily put her entire focus back on the Westmore case. If she wasn't going to get Josie back, her job had just tipped to the bordering-on-impossible-to-convict scale and she was absolutely not going to let that happen.

She studied what forensic evidence she had, looking for a perspective other than the obvious. And she did another deep dive into Lana's life. Looking for anyone or anything that she could use in court to prove that Wes Westmore had been abusing his girlfriend.

And she looked at him, too. Abusers usually didn't just start out with killing. There had to be things in his past. Had to be other women whom he'd mistreated. If only she could convince one of them to testify against him. Even friends who would know of his penchant for roughness could prove helpful.

Her job was to prosecute, but with a windbag like Mitch Mallard dragging his feet, she couldn't wait around for him to do the investigating, or trust that he'd be thorough.

She also had to keep her mind busy, her attention focused. She'd already lost control over her physical freedom; she would not give up say over her thoughts.

When sitting at the table in such close proximity to Cormac got to be too much, she went to her room. And when the walls there, blanketed by walls of snow on the street below, closed in, she went back out and settled on the couch he'd vacated.

She heard him go to the bathroom. Knew when he made coffee and pictured the cup at his mouth when his sips caught her attention. Remembered tasting that coffee-laced tongue.

And wondered a time or two what in the hell was wrong with her.

There'd been a popular sitcom, set right there in New York, where two of the female characters, during two different seasons, had been overly horny while pregnant and had put the condition down to stimulated hormones. But if she remembered right, both times the women had been in their fourth month. Not their second.

And who knew what kind of research those writers had done?

By late afternoon, she had done her own research. It wasn't like she could call her mom and ask. So she went on the internet.

She found some validation for her state. Apparently

libido increase was quite common, and sometimes present even before morning sickness. In the first trimester.

That didn't explain what had happened to her around Cormac two months before but, sitting there trapped by a stalker and a snowstorm, she went with the excuse and got back to work.

But then…dinner. They couldn't order takeout. And cooking two separate meals with both of them right there, hungry at the same time and sharing a small kitchen, seemed just plain stupid. Add that to the fact that Cormac's grocery supply was pretty much nonexistent and she had chicken breasts, rice and the rest of the ingredients necessary to make a baked dish she loved. She had to offer to cook for him, too. It was fair.

She made him dish up his own helping, though. And didn't set the table. He could grab a plate and fork, and land somewhere to eat on his own.

There was only one table. She brought her computer with her.

He had his.

And then he ruined things when, out of the blue, he said, "Wow, that was really good!"

Her own plate nearly empty, she looked up from her screen. Thinking his appreciative grin was the sexiest thing she'd ever seen, she flooded with warmth in her heart region, too.

"Thank you," she said, trying to be polite. Distant. But she didn't look away.

His expression sharpened. Grew serious.

"We need to talk."

No, they didn't. She didn't. She needed to work. But when he rounded the table, took a hold of her hand and tried to lead her from the table, she got up.

She grabbed for her plate, dropping his hand to reach for his plate as well. "The dishes," she said, and made a beeline for the kitchen.

He left her alone while she busied herself with the small bit of cleanup there was left.

Dare she hope he'd retired early for the night?

Did she really want him to have done so? Not sure she'd like the answer to the last question, she didn't dwell on it.

The question or the answer.

Because a greater one had surfaced. Again.

How could she possibly allow a man more than a decade younger than her to tie up his life with a woman who was going to be getting old a lot sooner than he was? A woman who was past her prime when he was right smack-dab in the middle of his?

How could she let herself get involved, romantically, at all? She knew where that led. Life would normalize. She'd get involved in a big case. She would forget important dates or moments, would come home with a briefcase full of work and would have nothing left to give when she crawled into bed at night.

The first time, she hadn't known herself well enough. Hadn't known how she'd be, or how important her work was to her sense of self-worth. She hadn't known how good she'd be at it, or how it fulfilled her.

After more than twenty years in the business, she knew it all too well. And would never be able to forgive herself for breaking another heart.

Which meant she had to shut her own down.

Except for the baby, of course. The way her heart leaped every time she allowed herself to think about actually carrying the child full term and giving birth, she knew that her baby would always be on her mind. Work or no.

Some kind of divine sense that God gave to mothers, she supposed.

And Cormac had, in a way, given the baby to her.

When she could stall no longer, kitchen counters all wiped clean and everything put away, she eyed her computer on the dining room table and made a beeline for it. Not even sure if he was still out in the living area of the apartment, she couldn't risk looking.

No eye contact. That was her new modus operandi.

Gaze on the computer. Only on the computer.

And then on the hand that was closing her computer. A strong, sexy male hand.

One that had been all over her body, had touched her most private places, fingers that had—

"We need to talk." Cormac's voice should have been like a blast of cold water to her want. She didn't even get that much of a break.

With her computer in hand, he walked over to the couch. Sat down.

Dare she hope they were going to talk about work?

She could refuse to join him. The laptop belonged to her. She could claim it, turn her back, walk down the hall, enter her room and lock the door.

Or just shut it. No way he'd force his way beyond a closed door. Not when there wasn't a bad guy beyond it, in any case.

But he was right. Definitely the more mature of the two of them at the moment. They had to reach some understandings where their child was concerned.

Sitting in the leather armchair that matched his couch, she glanced over at him, trying to figure out how to get him to drop the marriage idea once and for all. To come up with reasoning that would convince him how wrong such a union would be. To help him understand what she already knew.

She was trying valiantly not to notice the strong thighs accented by his tight jeans, and most definitely not to let her gaze travel up any higher.

Leaning forward, with his elbows on his knees, he rubbed his hands together. And she waited, still hoping he might be trying to figure out a way to break some bad news about Maxwell. Or the older guy, Kinney.

What did it say about her that she'd rather hear bad news about a stalker determined to take her, than talk about their future shared parenting of a child?

And about that...

"Have you told your siblings, or Sean at least, about being the baby's father yet?" Every time he'd been in touch with his brother in the past twenty-four hours, she'd wondered.

And worried.

She highly respected the decorated detective. She didn't want him thinking less of her because she'd fooled around with his younger brother.

"No." Cormac shook his head. Frowning. "I can't really do that until we've reached some decisions about how we're going to handle things between us. They're going to have questions."

Right. There was that. "Sorry," she said, glancing down at her own hands. "I...uh...don't have brothers and sisters. I'm not used to answering to anyone." Which was exactly as she wanted it. Needed it to be. Not at all sure how, with a baby in the picture, she was going to make that happen.

"The obvious solution here is for us to get married, Emily."

Her mouth flew open, the refusal rushing up to jump out, and Cormac took a hold of her hand.

The touch shouldn't have stopped her. Shouldn't have her heart pounding.

Was the man seriously going to propose a second time?

She had to snatch her hand back. Tell him no.

Get out.

Even if that meant being buried in the snow.

Except…she had a baby to think about. Couldn't risk freezing it to death.

She couldn't make all her choices based only on what she knew to be right for her.

Because it wasn't just her anymore.

"I can't marry a man I don't love." Cormac felt Emily's hand tremble in his as she said the words he'd expected to hear.

The words she'd said the first time he'd proposed marriage to her. He hadn't been ready for them then.

"You've said you're never going to fall in love again," he said. She'd spent days putting him off. He'd spent them vacillating between avoiding the situation and looking for the solution that had to be there, waiting for them to find it.

"That's right."

"Which means, you're never going to have that kind of traditional marriage."

"Yeah." Her frown didn't give any encouragement.

Lucky for them, he didn't need any. "So consider a different kind of marriage. One where you aren't in love with your husband. He knows it. Wants it that way. So you don't have to worry, ever again, about hurting someone like you hurt Paul."

She shook her head. But he shook his, too. "Hear me out, Em, please?"

Waiting for her agreement, knowing a lot rested on her ability to be open-minded to all sides of a story, he let out a long breath when she finally nodded.

He inhaled deeply. "We're both workaholics. We get consumed by the job, work impossibly long hours, and that's what makes us happy."

Her nod wasn't all that encouraging. He was on the easy part.

"And now we're going to have another human being who's fully dependent on the two of us. Night. Day. Weekends. And not just for food and clothes or doctor visits, but for companionship and guidance. Our job is going to include teaching right from wrong, self-discipline, compassion, how to brush teeth…even how to pee."

His gut clenched as he talked. And they'd have to teach the kid how to talk, too.

Ride a bike.

Bathe.

Overwhelmed for a second, he almost lost track of his mission. Emily's fingers within his moved, and he knew he couldn't fail.

Releasing her hand, he sat back. "I'm not going to settle for less than shared parenting," he blurted. Not at all what he'd meant to say next. He had it all thought out.

Had come up with the solution.

"I'm not asking you to."

Okay, well, good.

Really good.

He nodded. Lobbed his ankle over his opposite knee. Trying to convince himself he knew what he was doing.

He was going to be a father with full responsibilities. They'd established something.

Wow. He'd need…things. And he'd need to learn how to give a tiny kid a bath. How to change a diaper.

Hell, he'd never even *held* a baby.

Not since Eva. He'd been only six. And his parents had helped him.

Emily sat forward, bringing his attention to the breasts kind of pushed together between her arms. His baby was going to be…

"So, that's it?" she asked. "We're done here?"

What the hell! "No." he said, reining himself in to the case at hand. "We're just beginning." Especially since he was just figuring out how much help he was going to need. He'd been busy thinking about what having the baby would take out of her. Busy figuring out how to show her that she was going to need him.

Just getting himself in the picture.

He'd never actually jumped ahead to the finished product. Him fully in the picture.

"Like I was saying," he started in again, trying to get back to where he'd been when he'd started the conversation. "With both of us so committed to our jobs, we would better serve the kid by joining forces. Kind of pinch-hitting for each other for life," he continued, pulling on the hours he'd put into laying everything out for her.

"We get married, we just have one household to keep up. The kid has one room, one set of house rules, the same bed every night. The kid has the security of a solid home with one set of possessions. The kid has security.

Just the caregiver changes out as you and I work around and with each other, trading off parenting details as work requires. I work from home some, when I'm researching like I've been doing the past couple of days. You do the same, as you can."

It was all becoming clear again.

"I was planning on getting a nanny," she said.

A nanny. Even better. "Okay, good, so we do that, too, for the times when we both have to be out."

And those times when they were both in? Sharing a home?

Leaning forward again, he took her hand for a second time, rubbing his fingers along her palm as he knew turned her on. "On the easy side of it, we'd be able to quit fighting our base instincts and have sex together whenever we wanted," he added. He'd meant to smile. But met her serious gaze with a completely serious one of his own.

"You're assuming I still want it," she said, licking her lips as her gaze slid from his. Her voice filled with bravado.

"Your nipples are hard." If she hadn't wanted him to notice, she should have worn a padded bra under that sweater.

"It's frigid outside!"

He couldn't play games with her. Too much was at stake. "You're actually going to lie to me now?"

Those brown eyes moved until her gaze was locked with his again. "No," she said. "I'm dying over here with you in those jeans and me knowing in such detail what's beneath that fly."

It grew. To instant hardness.

But it wasn't time for sex. Even his penis seemed to get that one as it shrank again almost immediately.

"So it all makes sense, Em," he said. "People assume a couple marries, they're in love, but what we have—honesty, respect, the freedom to be married to our jobs, and adding in a home and family—it's the answer for us."

She shook her head again. So he moved forward. "Think outside the box," he urged, giving her the argument that had occurred to him in the middle of the night. "Isn't that what's made you such a great prosecutor? The fact that you look for what others aren't seeing. Same with me and my job. I look at everything, no matter how far-fetched, to find the truth, and let things fall where they fit. Well, this is what fits for us."

When Emily scooted closer, placing her hand on top of his, making a sandwich out of him, his heart started to pound. She was going to accept.

"We're both strong, determined people. Look at all we've accomplished, all we get done. If we set our minds to this, we'll get it done." He gave his closing argument.

Oh, God, she was going to agree.

Life as he'd known it would be no more. He'd be a married man, and—

"Answer me something," she said, instead of accepting his proposal. And his heart sank a bit again.

"Sure." He was up for whatever she had to hand out.

"What happens when you meet some other woman you want to have sex with?"

Or she met some other man she wanted, he translated. Emily wanted him, but not just him. She had her sights on someone else?

Or wanted the right to do so?

He sat there, speechless.
He hadn't thought things out closely enough.
He'd been blindsided.
And he wasn't even in love.

Chapter 19

Leaving Cormac speechless on the couch, unable to tell her that there wouldn't be any other women, Emily brewed herself a cup of chamomile tea, figuring she'd take it and her computer and escape to her room for the night.

Cormac was hot for her in the moment. It wasn't something that would last forever.

Hot sex rarely did.

That's where being in love came in to keep a marriage together.

Without it, their child was going to end up in a two-home, shared parenting life anyway. They might as well start out that way.

Save a whole bunch of hurt feelings.

Or at least prevent some of them. Feeling like she was going to cry, she dipped her tea bag in her cup, putting the emotionalism down to her out-of- whack hormones.

It turned out being pregnant was convenient as a scapegoat, too.

"Wait a minute." Cormac's words started in the living room but were coming toward her. "You don't get to point the finger at me to cover up for your own sexual desires," he said, coming out to stand in the doorway of the kitchen.

Effectively blocking her in.

She didn't feel threatened. The man would move if she barged toward him. What she felt was…threatened. In an entirely different way. How dare he stand there and try to force her to sit with her emotions.

If she didn't want to, she didn't have to.

The choice was hers.

"I'm not covering up my sexual desires," she told him. "I've admitted that I'm…attracted to you." She could have left it there. But the moment—the damned emotion—demanded more. "That I want you like I've never wanted anyone before in my life."

Okay, that was new. She'd never actually told him that.

But she couldn't deny it, either.

His eyes lit up, but he didn't come closer. He just braced his hands, shoulder-height, on both sides of the arch between the dining room and kitchen.

"You all but accused me of infidelity with some unknown woman in the future," he said. "Why not just come out and say that you don't see yourself being satisfied with only having sex with me for the rest of your life?"

Her mouth fell open. Again. She couldn't help it. "I… because… I can't imagine ever meeting another man who does it for me like you do." The words tumbled out of her through the shock. He couldn't be serious…

"I'm forty-three, Cormac. I've been around awhile.

Seen a lot of men. I'm pretty sure there's no one up ahead that's going to equal your charisma."

She hated being so much older than him.

He leaned into the kitchen more, his gaze brimming with emotion, and some pretty obvious fire, too, but he didn't let go of the wall. "So…you are accusing me of not having what it takes to be faithful to you."

Statement, not question. But she couldn't let it go unanswered. "Not accusing. That's the point. We aren't in love. It wouldn't be a traditional marriage. And have you seen yourself? You're about as gorgeous as…" She stopped. Couldn't go there anymore. "You exude sex appeal, Cormac. Women can't help but pursue that."

Herself included? Had she pursued him?

She remembered it more as him coming on to her, but…

Lips stiff, he looked put out. She hadn't meant to piss him off. And so the bald truth came pouring out. "I'm forty-three, Cormac." Yeah, they'd established that about a thousand times in the past few days. Or, she had, at least. "I'm going to be getting wrinkled long before you do. Less attractive. Stuff starts to sag, you know. And you…think about it. When I'm sixty, close to retirement, you're still going to be in your forties…climbing to bigger successes…"

"Pfft," he scoffed. "Are you kidding? No way you're retiring at sixty. If anything, you're going to be courting a judgeship. If you aren't there already."

A judgeship. She'd be lying if she didn't admit she'd thought about it. More than once. Something to fly on into her fifties and beyond.

But it wasn't an aspiration she'd ever spoken about. Not even out loud to herself.

And… "You're missing my point. Picture me at seventy. Forced into retirement. You'll be fifty-eight. Still out fighting crime. Even though you'll own an agency by then and have a staff of your own on the street. The fact is, I'll have aching bones and failing eyesight while you're still a happening power."

He shook his head. "I can picture you at ninety-five, if you'd like, to save time. I'll be eighty-four and you'll still be challenging me to be sharper, to figure things out so you don't figure them out for me. I figure we'll have equal wrinkles by then, if that makes you feel any better, and when I picture us lasting that long, as room-mates with benefits, I'm looking back on our fifty years together and not finding one boring minute among them."

He was going to kill her. Right then. Right there. Break her heart wide open and she'd be done.

To hell with stalkers. Or preeclampsia. Or hemorrhaging.

She was going to expire from a torn heart.

She couldn't die. She had a baby on the way. A miracle she'd never thought to experience. No way she was going to miss it.

She was going to need help.

The baby had a father. Deserved to be fully loved by him.

Emily had to defend her heart against him. To save herself. And him.

Out of nowhere, the solution appeared.

She looked at him and said, "How about if we just live together?"

He wanted it legal.

The immediate response startled Cormac—loner that he was. Having an out as simple as moving if things weren't working did seem like the perfect solution.

Yeah, it meant that anytime Emily decided he was too much of a pain in the ass, she could just pack up herself and his kid and go, but…

"Okay."

Holy hell!

She'd agreed to be with him. Full-time.

The ramifications…he couldn't even start…where… when…moving…boundaries between them…loss of independence…no space of his own… Emily to come home to, coming home to him…being there to watch his kid grow inside her…living full-time with the kid after birth…blind…blind…blind.

"Okay? You sure?"

No. His mind was reeling. But he said, "Yeah, I'm sure," the words carrying a truth he wasn't sure he understood.

He got the body language, though. As Emily met his gaze, smiling, he was instantly hard. And didn't turn away. That look…alluring, tempting, promising and needy, too…he hadn't seen it in full force for two long months.

But he had been dreaming about it ever since.

"And as soon as you find yourself wanting sex with another woman, you tell me and we move to separate bedrooms," she said. The prosecutor laying out her case. Firm. In control.

If you didn't count the way she was moistening her lips. And those nipples…hard through the sweater.

When had he become obsessed with breasts?

Her breasts.

He wasn't going to be the one to bring infidelity into their home. But…whatever.

"Fine."

"I mean it, Cormac. The sex has to be monogamous or not at all."

The sex. Now, that he could sign on for. He nodded.

And…she hadn't said she'd move out if he found someone else, she'd just move bedrooms. Or he would.

It was all a little much. There'd been no one serious since Willa, not because there weren't offers, but because he had the life he wanted.

But now there was a kid coming.

And the mother…

He definitely wanted to be there for her in any way he could, to have her close so he knew when she needed help, and to have his kid growing up living with him.

Mostly what he wanted in that moment was to scoop up the most incredible woman he'd ever slept with and carry her down the hall. To leave behind everything else—the worries, the dangers, the changes, the cases, the questions—and lose himself in her.

Which was exactly why he'd broken up with her.

"I know it's not what either of us chose for our lives," he said slowly. "But I really do believe that if anyone can make this situation work, it's us."

"You're really going to push this," she said, and he wondered if she'd been messing with him when she'd suggested living together. Challenging him.

Calling his bluff?

What the hell, she hadn't been serious about suggesting they live together?

"We're too independent, too used to doing things our own ways, Cormac."

"A baby doesn't fit in either of our lives," he countered. Two could play that game.

When she didn't argue, he moved a little closer to her. "Our independence is what's going to make this work, Em. Because we're equally that way. We aren't going to need from each other what most people look to get from their spouses."

He almost convinced himself.

He'd get there.

"And it doesn't feel to you like there's something missing?"

He didn't know what he felt. Wasn't used to checking in with emotional stuff.

"It feels like we're coming up with the solution that fits us, and will serve our baby the best."

He'd rather she marry him. Make it legally official. In case of emergency or whatever else he wasn't coming up with right now.

"No sense in buying two cribs, two high chairs, I guess," she said then. "But if you do meet someone, or you just want out, you have to promise to be honest about it. To let me know. I give you my word you would still have shared parenting and full say in the baby's life."

Her penchant for him to be with someone else was beginning to annoy him.

A lot.

It was like she was trying to push him off on someone else…

Just like with the age stuff…

Unless—what if she was the one who had doubts about being fulfilled with someone so much younger than she was?

Could be that when she reached an age where she

wanted to retire, she wanted to be with someone who was at that same point in life?

Or when she started to show her age, her partner did, too?

Maybe she thought some guy in his mid-forties would be more mature than Cormac was.

Growing cold inside, he stared at her. Had she just been playing with him two months before? Was he a damned boy toy?

Shaking his head, he dismissed the thought even as it occurred to him. There'd been nothing lopsided about his relationship with Emily. They'd been equals in every sense.

He'd bet his life on that one.

But...

Staring at her, he understood what she'd been trying to tell him.

They might know what was and wasn't inside their relationship, but others would have their own ideas. Some would judge.

"Would you like to tell the world that we're just roommates?" he asked, needing a beer. He was unable to fathom how life had careened so far out of control.

"What would be the point? Everyone's going to know that you're the father of my child."

Right.

His siblings were going to have a hard time believing that one.

He was watching her, trying like hell to come up with something. He was the guy who found the answers. It was his thing.

When her eyes started to fill, he thought it was the light at first. Some weird glow coming from...nowhere. The closest light was the dining room behind them.

"Em?"

She blinked. Smiled. Which drew his attention to the fact that her lips were trembling. She shook her head.

And a tear dropped to her cheek.

"I'm sorry," she said, standing and then turning toward the hall.

"Hey." He stood, too. Reached for her hand and when she didn't yank it back, pulled her toward the couch with him. He sat close beside her as she dropped down, but not close enough to touch.

"We'll get through this," he told her, certain of that one.

She nodded.

"Yeah, you're the one doing the physical work, but I'm going to shoulder this every bit as much."

And he shouldn't be pressuring her.

She nodded again, wiping her eyes. But the tears hadn't stopped.

"Look, whatever way you want it to go, that's what we'll do."

Another nod. He didn't seem to be helping at all.

"Talk to me, Em."

"It's just hormones."

Somehow, he doubted that. But he chose to keep the opinion to himself.

With a sob that became half shudder, she looked at him, shaking her head again. "I just can't make sense of this week," she said. "Nearly being kidnapped, finding out the guy's so sick he's stalking me. And spying on us. I'm afraid to go outside. I've got this jerk of a detective on the case of my career, and a witness who's skipped. And… I'm pregnant?"

Nodding, he ran his hand through her hair. Just to touch her. For him. For her.

"Just when you think you've got life under control and firmly in your grasp, it throws you a curve ball," he said. He ought to know. He'd been lobbing them since his mother died. And then, at just fourteen, when his father passed.

She moved her face into the hand at her hair. Just closed her eyes and held him with her cheek. He remained steady, needing to be just whatever she needed in that moment. He didn't worry about himself getting through whatever came.

He'd mastered that one.

But her...carrying a child that you find out you really want and fearing that your body won't cooperate. That alone would be enough to unhinge a person.

And if she continued with a healthy pregnancy, in a few months, everywhere she went, people would know her secret. They were only going to know his if he told them.

Her face moved inward, until her lips were touching his palm. His other hand raised to support the back of her head, intending to help her take whatever comfort she needed.

"Make love to me, Cormac."

He barely heard the words at first. Wasn't sure they weren't just a figment of his own desire.

"Take me to our place...just long enough for me to find myself again..."

She'd stopped kissing his flesh. Was staring straight into his eyes, her gaze wide-open. Clear.

"Please."

"I won't apologize in the morning," he told her, his voice thick with the need he'd been aching with all week.

"I won't ask you to."

She leaned in then, her lips meeting his, and he lost whatever restraint he might have hoped he'd have.

Picking her up, he carried her down the hall to his bed.

Chapter 20

For the first time all week, Emily was doing exactly what she wanted to do. Stretched out on Cormac's sheet, she teased him about his unmade bed.

Something she'd done the first time she'd been there, two months before.

And when he ground his still-clothed groin against her thigh, she lit on fire like she'd never known she could do—until him.

And laughed a little because, in spite of everything, he still turned her on that much.

"I need to feel good," she said, licking his neck as she reached for the bottom of his shirt. "Too much bad…"

He sat up, and for a second, she was afraid.

It wasn't working for him anymore.

Her. The baby.

He'd been hard as a rock, but…

He'd pulled off his shirt. "I don't mean to be crass, but I have to relieve some pressure here," he said, undoing the fly of his jeans.

Her body soared again. Heart and soul. Except that she didn't do those things. Physically it soared to the sky. Waiting for him to send the fireworks up to join her.

"Being crass never stopped you in the past," she murmured.

"Yeah, I'm trying for a little more decorum this time around." He'd stripped, completely naked, was right there for her to see his passion, and fell down beside her.

And she laughed again. She had forgotten just how glorious he'd made her feel. Even before the sex.

She'd have stripped for him, right then, right there, as fast as she could, would have crawled right up on him, but she knew he liked to undress her piece by piece.

And she needed his special touch.

Oh, how she needed it.

"This could take a while," he said, his lips following his fingers as he raised the bottom of her sweater, and she took on the sexy chills he sent through her.

"Take all the time you need," she said, shivering with delight.

She'd never met a man who got off on enjoying every inch of a woman's body. Who was hard enough to explode, but had the control to put himself on hold until she was as ready as he was.

"You have no idea how many times the past two months I wished I'd taken a picture of this," he said when her breasts finally sprang free of the front closure on her unlined bra.

She'd never had such a complete lack of self-consciousness, of shyness, around a man.

"As I recall, you said you didn't want any to exist so they didn't ever fall into wrong hands."

She'd teased him about being, always, the private investigator.

"I was stupid."

Anything but. Still, she smiled.

By the time he had her pants off, she'd pretty much lost any control she had over her own need. Legs spread for him, she urged him forward.

"I'm going to need more than once," he burst out hoarsely as he entered her.

In the past, she'd closed her eyes during the ride, so caught up in the explosion there was nothing but that.

But as he entered her, his throat thick with his need, she watched him, the way his face creased with exertion, the sweat on his shoulders, and up, to see his gorgeous dark eyes looking straight at her.

Filled with intensity, that gaze held her captive as his body caressed hers from the inside out, and back in again.

And when she came, when he poured into her, their gazes were still locked.

She'd never have believed any orgasm would be better than those she'd experienced during that incredible December week.

But it was.

And when he lay down beside her, just watching her, with that satisfied grin on his face, she'd never felt so beautiful, either.

Cormac woke sometime in the middle of the night, brought from a deep sleep by soft, silent movement in his bed. But he wasn't coherent enough to figure out what it was until Emily was already off the bed and heading toward his door.

Going to her own room, to sleep in her own bed, he knew.

He got it.

Given their current circumstances, if he'd woken after sex in her bed, he'd have done the same thing. People who knew they couldn't give in to a rash of emotion, who knew that to do so put others at risk, had a particular set of challenges in life.

Whatever ironic twist of fate had given two such people an unplanned baby to raise—most particularly after said couple took precautions to make certain that didn't happen—was a fate he hoped to never meet again.

A fate he loathed.

He already loved and wanted that baby. And had to make damned sure he didn't follow suit with the mother.

Getting emotionally hooked on Emily would ruin everything. For both of them.

She'd never go for it. Or let herself love him back even if she fell for him. And there he'd be, blind in love and missing the nuances that he needed to see to keep them all safe, while she focused on work and the kid.

She was who he wanted to be when he grew up...

The thought occurred and he knew instantly how false it was. It might be what she thought, but there was no way he was anything but on an equal par with Emily Hernandez.

And still overpumped from the night and its necessary ending, he started right in with his defense when he came out the next morning, in jeans and another sweater, and saw her already at work at the table, tea and a partially eaten croissant beside her.

As though it was any other morning.

"Yeah, you've lived longer than I have," he said, just continuing his thought process aloud as he turned on the one cup serving size of coffee, and stood in the archway to the dining room, arms crossed.

Clearly startled, she glanced over at him, eyes wide.

He could have handled the moment better. Took a second to regroup and get where he was going without emotion attached.

"You heading somewhere with that?" she asked, seemingly nonchalant, but the little pulse in her neck that he'd teased her about in the past...it was in high gear.

"I am," he told her, leaning against the arch, crossing his feet, his concession to unemotional delivery. "You've lived longer, but I'd wager my retirement on the number of life experiences I've crammed into mine, as opposed to you and yours."

She stiffened, and he straightened. Still not stellar communication skills, but he had the winning point.

"You say you grew up with a basically idyllic childhood."

"Other than being an only child, so used to going it alone a lot, yeah, I did. My folks were in love, *are* in love. My dad was a cop, so Mom and I worried sometimes, but he always made it home safely. We took wonderful family vacations every year. Always to someplace different. If you think because I grew up in New York and have always lived here, that I haven't seen the world—"

"Not where I'm going at all," Cormac said, taking a moment to retrieve his coffee. He couldn't suddenly sprout years to equal hers. And those years between them seemed to bother her a lot.

Why he was picking on them, when there were so

many other things standing in their way, he didn't know. Maybe because it was a battle he actually thought he could win.

Or one he could more easily handle.

The snow had dissipated some. The cocoon that had kept them safe the day before was melting. If she decided to go out, he couldn't stop her. Maxwell was still on the loose, denying that he was the woman on the tapes, and they were waiting on a warrant to search his place and vehicle, hopefully later this morning. They didn't have enough on James Kinney to do anything with him, either. Other than keep watch.

"Your biggest challenge growing up was not having a sibling. Mine was not having a mother. And having to share one parent with three other siblings. Then Dad got cancer. His death was slower. We had to watch it happen. And at fourteen, I had to say goodbye to him, too. Sean did great, keeping us together, and Humphrey was a godsend, but we were living in a house with an eighteen-year-old being the most experienced among us. We all learned quickly. Stepped up beyond our years. And then Liam took a wrong path. I watched my twin go to prison..."

She was staring at him. Realizing that what he was doing was dangerously akin to spilling his guts, Cormac sat down at the end of the table. "I'm not crying about any of this, though it does maybe seem that way," he acknowledged. "I'm just presenting facts, truth, to prove my point," he continued. "I'm going to need my retirement to pay for the kid's college."

She didn't smile.

"If you measure age by life experience, rather than

breaths taken on earth, I'd say we're pretty neck and neck," he finished, pushing his truth home.

When she took a sip of tea and then licked her lips, he wanted to kiss her.

And he didn't want to muck up their waters anymore. They had the sex down pat. It had never been a problem between them.

But there were problems.

Maybe unsurmountable ones.

They had to find a way to surmount them well enough to live together and raise a healthy and happy kid.

It took him a second to realize that Emily wasn't arguing with him. Wasn't shaking her head or crossing her arms, or even getting that tense defensive look on her face.

She sat there in tight black pants and a midthigh-length, black-and-white, high-collared sweater and tapped her finger on the table.

He'd seen her tap her finger like that once before, when he'd sat in a courtroom and watched her work a case he wasn't involved in. He'd stopped by the courthouse to meet her to discuss the case they'd shared. Court had run over.

She'd been presented evidence that had just turned up. Had been mulling her options, determining what kind of deal she could make to see that the defendant still paid for her crime.

He'd won.

The point.

Thinking quickly, so he'd be prepared when she was presented her offer, he determined how low his bar could go.

Living together. That was it.

As low as he was willing to negotiate.

Seeing that it was an offer she'd already put on the table, Cormac sipped his coffee, satisfied with the day's work.

And it was barely past dawn.

"Life isn't just measured by past experiences." Not sure what she was fighting for, Emily knew she had to state her case. She and Cormac, they were so good, so powerful together, when it came to work.

And sex.

And now they were going to be raising a baby together. If they didn't acknowledge the challenges they were facing, deal with them, those challenges could implode three lives.

She gave the facts another mental replay. They were workaholics who put career first because it made them happiest, but also because they knew that if they didn't, other people got hurt. Neither of them ever wanted another one-on-one committed full-time relationship.

A real marriage.

And…she was a lot older than he was. Would age before he did.

He was in his prime and she was heading for the midlife crisis years.

Oh, good Lord, was that what she was having? An early onset midlife crisis?

Scared for a second there, afraid she'd screwed up worse than ever before, she went back two months as her mind raced to catalog facts.

And no…definitely no. Cormac Colton was no crisis.

He'd been…perfect for her. Her sexual fantasy. Her freedom to live deeply and completely in surreal hours with someone who also only wanted those hours. Not forever.

He'd been her gift to herself.

And right now he was saying nothing. He wasn't sipping coffee anymore, either. He just sat there, waiting. Which was his way.

Cormac would gather the facts, ferret out the truth and then move in for the takedown.

Or the save.

One of the many things she admired about him.

"It's not just the living we've done, but the life ahead," she said slowly. Feeling as though three lives were on the brink and only she could save them. "Jump ahead for a second," she said, as though leading a jury. "We have the baby. You excel at the whole fatherhood thing." Because whether he saw it in himself yet or not, she knew he would.

Which was why she couldn't even think about depriving her child of the privilege of being raised by him.

"A few years down the road, you've got the hang of it, and you want to have another go at it."

A reasonable assumption. Happened more often than not.

He held up a hand. Shook his head. "Let's get through what's directly in front of us and not borrow trouble from the future," he said. "One baby at a time."

Of course. In ordinary circumstances, she'd agree so completely she'd never even have had the thought. "The point is that if you're tied to me, then you don't get that choice, Cormac. Because my life is rounding the curve to no longer being capable of bearing children. I don't have the few years to give. You do."

It was such a glaringly clear fact.

"You sure that's what you want to go with?" he asked, his look so intent his brow was raised and creased.

Not quite as sure of herself in light of his seeming confidence, she nodded. How in the hell did he do that? Make her doubt what she knew?

Always challenging her to see more when so many others just took for granted that she'd get it right. And that she'd get there more quickly than many.

Because she had no life to distract her from the case at hand.

"Yes, I'm sure," she said aloud, when he seemed to be waiting for verbal confirmation. Needing to be out from beneath his supreme Cormac Colton microscope.

"Okay, so let's go and jump ahead for a second." He repeated her own words back at her. "Let's jump to, I don't know, the kid's in high school, ready to graduate, and I don't want to be done. I want to have another…"

Exactly. High school might be a little late for many, but…

"Because that happens, too, you know."

She conceded with another nod.

"And, just to even the score, let's say you're my age now. Thirty-two just like me."

Then he had no point. Was arguing a different case.

"Let's add eighteen years to the thirty-two and what have we got? Hmm…right, fifty. Check me on that. My math and all."

She heard the facetiousness loud and clear. Did not at all see how the picture he was painting had anything at all to do with her being too old for him.

Pushing his cup aside with his forearm, he leaned on the table, facing her. Those lips…for a brief moment there, she got lost in the memory of them on hers the night before, right after he'd come a second time...

"You with me yet?" he asked.

She almost shook her head. But stopped. Thought.

And he said, "I could be seventy and want another kid. You could be fifty, Em, twenty years younger than me, and I could still father a child, but you wouldn't be able to conceive it for me. It's not my doing, it's just the way life is."

Okay. He had a point. But it was stretched way thin.

"By your theory, then, a woman who can't have children at all...where does she fit? Because if she marries a man who, sometime down the road, decides he wants to have a child after all, she'd be holding him back just like you're holding me back, right?"

That wasn't fair. To women who couldn't conceive first and foremost.

"Life gives us things we can't change," he finally said. "My parents dying. You being born eleven years before me. They're challenges. We all get them in one form or another."

Yes, but... "You had no say or control over your parents' deaths, just as I had nothing to do with when I was born. But this—" she pointed between the two of them "—this we can stop."

That look again, so intense. "Can we?"

"Of course we can. You proved that two months ago. And might I remind you, it was your choice back then. Not mine."

"Can we stop the fact that we created a baby together?"

Ahh. Good moves.

He'd won that round.

"You want to change that circumstance?" he asked.

"Of course not." The baby. Not his win. She'd entertain options for objecting to that one if she could come up with any.

And, anyway, what was he getting at? What had he won? They were back where they'd already been. Living together. They'd already decided.

"All I'm saying here is that the age thing...it's not an issue for me."

Oh.

No reason for her to feel warmer suddenly.

But she did.

Chapter 21

Cormac had to go out. Ostensibly because he was meeting his siblings at Humphrey's Upper West Side apartment. But even if the appointment hadn't come up later that morning, with Ciara being free to spend some time with them because of the storm, he probably would have found another reason. He needed time out of his old space, away from the woman who'd turned his life completely on its axis, to find himself.

No more letting Emily twist him up. By the time he returned to her, he'd have himself firmly in check again.

Permanently. He'd managed the emotions she'd raised in him two months before. He could do so again.

Then, it had been only to save her and himself. Now, with the baby involved, the need was ever more crucial. He and Emily had to be able to talk about tough stuff without him getting all feely inside.

With full details watching his place, outside, door, elevators, his floor, he felt mostly under control by the time he stood at the big window in Humphrey's apartment looking out at the view. The white encasing the city hid so much…

"I thought you all would like to see this," Ciara said, handing Sean an old photo album. Ready to be fully focused on work, Cormac joined Eva on one side of his older brother, while Liam was on the other.

"It's all of us." Eva sounded pleased, pointing to a photo of herself, at six, sitting alone on a motorcycle that belonged to one of their dad's fellow PIs. As Sean turned the pages, Cormac watched how the changes came over the four of them after their father died and Humphrey stepped in with the guidance and help Sean needed to keep them all together.

They'd grown more serious. Less starry-eyed.

Even little Eva.

Every Christmas, though, Humphrey had been with them. And they'd all had smiles on their faces then.

Peering over Liam's shoulder, Ciara said, "I felt bad last Christmas, keeping him from you all." They'd just gotten married. It was understandable.

Things changed.

People changed.

No matter how old or young they were.

Had Humphrey changed so much that they didn't really know him anymore?

Ever since he met Ciara…

It's like Cormac had told Emily, age wasn't what mattered in life. It all came down to who you were, what you'd learned and who you knew.

When Ciara turned away, Cormac thought he saw tears

in her eyes. He didn't want to put her on the spot with his siblings and him all looking on, but when she turned back around, his gut clenched.

"I have a confession to make…"

She'd killed Humphrey.

Or knew who had.

Had she hired someone to have him killed?

The young wife coming into a goodly amount of money?

All three of his siblings were staring at her. Was the woman nuts, thinking she was going to come clean with all of them there, and have them just be calm about it?

No one moved. Or seemed to breathe.

He was opening his mouth to suggest they move their little party down to the precinct, when Ciara blurted, "My marriage to Humphrey…it's not real."

"What do you mean it's not real?" Wearing his most intimidating frown, Sean pinned Ciara with a stare similar to the ones the rest of them were nailing into her.

"It's not legal?" Liam asked.

"It's legal." The green eyes looking back at them were filled with emotions Cormac couldn't immediately decipher. But he didn't see guilt there.

Worry, though, that was definitely present. "Tell us," he urged.

What had she gotten his uncle into?

"Humphrey and I…we weren't in love. He did me a favor by marrying me. It's a marriage of convenience. We've never even slept together."

So marriages did happen without love. Cormac's first thought came and went. "What favor did he do for you?" Sean asked, just as Cormac had been about to.

"What trouble did you get him into?" he asked instead.

Damn the woman! She could have told them this from the beginning.

"It's nothing to do with his disappearance," Ciara said quickly, eyes wide now as she looked between the four of them. "Believe me, I care about Humphrey a lot. If I thought for one second that…" She shook her head.

"Why don't you let us be the judge of that?" Liam stepped toward her. Cormac followed suit, but whether it was to restrain his twin if need be, or to help him, he wasn't sure.

Liam had been seeing Humphrey…relying on him… needing him. He stood to lose more than just an honorary uncle.

"No!" Ciara was crying as she shook her head. "I can't talk about it right now. It's…about me…my life. Humphrey did me a favor is all. I'm just… I'm sorry that I took him from you at Christmastime." She nodded toward the photo album. "You're a family and…"

She spun around and ran. Seconds later, the living room resonated with the sound of a door closing, followed by the click of a lock.

Looking from one to another of his siblings, Cormac couldn't find his usual detachment, his unemotional way of viewing the facts to figure out what was real and what was subterfuge.

When Liam moved to follow Humphrey's young wife, Sean held him back with a hand to his shoulder. "Let her go. We need to look into her more. Discreetly. Which means mostly you, Cormac. Find out what possible reason a marriage to Humphrey would have helped her. Could be as simple as she had to be married to stay in the country."

Ciara most definitely didn't appear anything but American. Her dress, her accent, but Cormac got Sean's take, and agreed with it. "We don't want to cause more trouble, or draw attention to her or Humphrey, if she hasn't done anything illegal," he added, watching while Liam and Eva nodded.

"Not until we know more about what's going on." Sean dropped the photo album to the coffee table. Cormac, seeing it sit there, felt another peculiar pang.

He didn't want to leave their precious memories with Ciara.

But he had no right to take any of Humphrey's possessions with the man still presumed to be alive.

Nothing that wasn't pertinent to the case, at any rate.

"I...uh...have a secret to confess as well." He heard the words. Felt them come up from his throat and out of his mouth.

He had made no conscious, well-thought-out decision to speak them. But he couldn't seem to stop their rush to escape, either.

Not even when all three of his siblings pinned him with their implacable stares.

"Emily Hernandez's baby..." They all three nodded, seeming more confused than anything. Not surprising when he caught a glimpse of himself from the outside looking in.

Who was this guy?

"It's mine."

A sharp intake of breath came at him. Both of his brothers spoke at once. A "what the hell" and a "no way." All Cormac focused on was Eva. Eyes wide, mouth open, she stared at him.

Her eyes filled with tears. And she hugged him.

"You and Emily Hernandez?" she squealed, pulling away to look up at him.

Her shock unhinged him a bit. Because it didn't seem to be about the baby so much as about the woman he'd made it with. Was that what Emily had been talking to him about? The way others would react to them together—the older woman with the younger man? Were people really going to make an issue out of something that mattered not at all?

"I can't believe this! Emily Hernandez and a baby, but it's perfect!" Eva said then. "From everything I've heard and now have seen in the past couple of days, she's as much into her work as you are. And as smart and good at it, too. It makes sense that it would take someone like her, as strong as you, to…"

To what? He needed to know.

Instead, he fell forward half a step as Sean clasped his shoulder and gave it a squeeze. "Gotta admit, I didn't see this coming, but wow, man, that's going to be one lucky kid."

No shock about Emily?

"I pity him if he even thinks about stepping out of line," Liam said then, giving him a playful punch to the shoulder. "He'll be the kid with the father who has bionic vision," his twin continued. "Take it from me, trying to pull things off without you knowing about them is no easy feat."

What in the hell was Liam talking about? "You did it."

"Sweating bullets. And only because we were apart enough that I could manage to hide things…until I couldn't."

Yeah, Cormac had been instrumental in that part.

But before that? His brother had had to try to keep

Cormac from catching on to his illegal missteps? He'd thought Liam had been leaving him clues all along, silently asking for help, and that he'd just missed them all.

"Shut up, you guys," Eva said. "Cormac's going to be a wuss as a dad. The best dad ever, but that kid will be walking all over him, you wait and see…"

It was like he'd stepped into a twilight zone. Again. Every day, the world he'd known was becoming more surreal.

No one asked if he and Emily were going to get married. Maybe they assumed it would happen. Maybe they were afraid to find out.

Either way, Cormac got the hell out of there before he could lose any more pieces of the man he knew himself to be.

Or take on any more parts of this guy his siblings saw, but he didn't.

Eva had had it right when she'd said he was into his work.

Everyone just needed to leave it at that.

Emily had left her file of crime scene photos at the office. She had digital copies on her computer, but the originals were larger than she could print. She'd had them blown up so that she could take them home, pin them on the case board in one of her bedrooms and study them.

They'd only arrived the morning of the abduction and she hadn't even opened them. She'd also failed to bring the original photos she had for another case—photos that the owner had asked not to be reproduced and to be returned when she was through with them. That case, an abuse case, would be going to trial the following month and she had no idea how long she was going to be cooped up, hiding from a deranged man who thought her baby was magically going to be his.

The absurdity of that thought had her thinking of Eugene Maxwell again. There was no man in her life, no one who'd have even half an idea that she'd want to go out with him, let alone have his baby, and while Maxwell didn't know that, the man was diabolical in how he'd played his hand with her. Played with her head.

Preying on her where she was most vulnerable.

Because he believed she'd hit him in the exact same place.

So, she figured, in a twisted sense, they were having something together: mental anguish.

She'd texted Cormac to let him know she was going to the office, with police protection, and heard back from him that he was already on his way home, asking that she wait to let him go with her, saving the city a little money, but more, he wanted to talk to her.

Figuring that his conversation was work related, since he was coming from a meeting with his siblings on the Humphrey case, she waited.

She would be lying if she didn't admit to herself that she'd rather have him protecting her than anyone else. Not so much because he was the father of her baby, but because he was Cormac. He made every job personal. Gave his life to it.

As soon as they were safely ensconced in the private car he'd hired to drive him that day, given the snow and security issues, he rolled up the window between them and the driver and told her about Ciara's confession.

She'd been right, he'd had news on the case.

Surprising news.

Throughout the drive and the ride up in the elevator to her office, they discussed possibilities. She had several to suggest, for which he thanked her, saying he'd follow up as soon as they got home. It was possible that Ciara's family had had some means to force her, emotionally, into a marriage she didn't want. That she'd been seeing Humphrey secretly, and that he'd chosen to marry her to stop the abuse.

That sounded exactly like something Humphrey Kelly would do, he'd said.

So he'd be doing another deep dive on social media some time that night, looking through all of Ciara's accounts and friend lists.

Which, if she had a couple of thousand friends, which so many people did, would be a hell of a lot of profiles for him to weed through.

And that was good.

Because it meant no time for a repeat of the night before.

Emily had something to talk to him about, too.

She couldn't have sex with him again until they'd reached a final settlement regarding their immediate future.

She wasn't into a trying-on stage. Wasn't sure she could afford the effort.

Or the emotional cost.

She couldn't take on another breakup.

"I told my siblings about the baby."

She froze, file in hand halfway pulled out of her drawer, and looked up at him.

She'd told him to do it. But she had thought she'd at least get a heads-up.

And…the look in his eye…like he was…seeking something. Not from her.

But showing her he needed it, maybe?

"Were they supportive?" she asked. What they thought of her didn't matter to her, but they were his family, his whole life.

"Completely," he told her, still looking somewhat outside of himself.

His answer shocked her. "They know it's me having it?"

"Of course. They know you're pregnant. Sean's working your case. I told them I was the father of your baby. I didn't have any plan to do so or I would have warned you. It just happened."

He didn't sound defensive. Or even as though he was explaining himself.

More like, needing to know himself why he'd done what he had.

She didn't have that answer. She hadn't felt so moved where her own parents were concerned so couldn't relate.

She envied him, though. Having it done.

She wondered if age differences came up, but she didn't ask.

Didn't want to put him on the spot of having to hurt her feelings or worry her, since she was, apparently, the only one of the two of them who even thought the eleven years between them was an issue.

His text app sounded. The same sound he'd been using in early December. And all week long.

He read. Read again.

And glanced up at her, eyebrows raised, as he dialed his phone.

"Sean, yeah, what's…"

In the silence, she watched expressions chase themselves across Cormac's face as he listened to his older brother. Set her file on top of the large mailer envelope that contained the crime scene photos she'd come for.

It could be his brother was warning him about getting more involved with Emily. Looking out for his younger brother. Saving him from being trapped by a single woman whose biological clock was almost done ticking.

But more likely, Sean had news pursuant to the Humphrey Kelly meeting the siblings had just come from. Reporting on some action item that had resulted from said gathering.

Whatever news Sean was imparting, Cormac listened intently, frowned a lot. Glanced at her a time or two. After a couple of long minutes, he said, "Yeah, I will, keep me posted," and hung up.

"Eugene Maxwell is on the loose. They made his cover, but he managed to get away from the officers who saw him. He's armed with at least two handguns. The warrant came through to search his apartment and they found a spiral-bound notebook explaining why he was doing what he was doing."

Unable to swallow past the dryness in her throat, looking around the room for a place to hide—or escape—and finding neither, she asked the smart question. The one she didn't want to hear answered. "And that is?"

"He's going to kill you, his wife and her current husband. He doesn't care if he dies in the process. He can't stand the thought of the three of you living and loving, being happy, while leaving him to clean other people's trash. He'd lived an honorable, respectable life, fighting hard to get his college degree, to be a good husband, father and extended family member. It all ended when the man who killed his cousin was set free. According to his journal, the man taunted him outside the courthouse the day he walked."

She had no words. Could see it all as though she'd laid out the case herself.

"We're to shelter here until further notice," he said then. The security at the DA's office is better than anywhere we might try to take you. Court was canceled today due to the storm so there aren't a lot of people in the area, other than the police presence that is slowly filling in downstairs."

"He's coming for me first?"

"That's what the journal said, but SWAT's been dispatched to his wife's home as well. Chances are, he doesn't know you're here. But we don't know how closely he's been following your movements. Or how, for that matter."

The man had seen them outside a baby store and they still didn't know how.

"What if he's already here? Already inside?" She couldn't see beyond her four walls and door. No windows into the hallway.

"Then trying to leave would be extremely dangerous." He told her what she already knew. "All floors are being searched as we speak," Cormac said, ushering her into her bathroom, locking the door and putting her in the corner behind him. Without another word, or even looking at her, he positioned himself along the wall, to the left of the door, gun raised. If anyone shot through the door, the bullets would miss them both.

And if someone came through the door, Cormac would have a good chance of getting him before he got them.

She knew the facts. Could see them unfolding right in front of her.

And had never felt less in control, or more helpless, in her life.

Chapter 22

He stood ready, sweating like he'd never sweated before. His… Emily. His child. He'd die before he let the fiend get to them. The terror had to end.

The woman was trying to grow a baby she desperately wanted. Odds were less in her favor than most. No way anyone was going to get in the way of that.

Emily was having a kid *he* desperately wanted.

The thought hit him as his phone, which he'd set to silent, vibrated against his leg.

Gun still at the ready, he pulled the phone from his pocket with his left hand. Quickly scrolled.

And slid down the wall to the floor.

"What?" Emily's harsh question brought some of the blood back to his veins.

"He's in custody," he told her. And then gave her the rest that he had. "His ex-wife and her husband are dead. My address was typed into the GPS on his phone."

That was it. All he had. Relief flooded him.

"He didn't know we were here, at my office," she said. "But he knew I was staying with you."

It made sense, Maxwell *had* been following her. Just not that morning. Because he'd been busy committing murder elsewhere in the city.

Turning his head along the wall, he met her gaze, as she sat back looking at him. One wall, two heads.

And life was good.

"I can go home." The way her legs were shaking, Emily wasn't quite ready to stand up yet.

"You said we'd live together." Cormac's tone still carried a good bit of tension. She didn't blame him. She had heard about people being hunted. Had prosecuted the hunters.

But she'd never been a target.

It put a whole different spin on life.

He was waiting for an answer. "I meant after the baby was born," she said the words, but looked away. She wasn't ready.

Was still feeling stalked.

"I meant starting now." He didn't sound ready to compromise. "You might need to go on bed rest," he reminded her. "You'll need me around to help out." She hadn't actually said that part to him, but it made sense that he'd figured it out. "And it also stands to reason that you can't embark on a moving expedition while on bed rest. In addition, since the bed rest requirement isn't a preplanned thing, you'll have no way of knowing when that time could be. Which leads us to conclude that the moving should happen now."

She scrambled for an answering argument. "Your place is too small."

"And yours doesn't have enough bedrooms for an office, a baby room, and a spare bedroom, in the event you want your own place to sleep and kick me out of the master. It would do for now, but then I would have to move twice." He sounded as though he wasn't into that at all. And she couldn't blame him. "I want permanency. If you won't marry me, I at least have to have a mutual, long-term home with both our names on the lease."

Too much. She was still sitting on the floor with weak limbs.

And she had no argument to offer. What he said made sense.

All of it.

"I guess we need to go apartment hunting," he said then. Standing.

"Right now?" she asked, reminding herself they were going to be roommates, not a couple, as she took the hand he offered her and stood up.

Even if they'd been married, it would have been that way. It was what he wanted. What they both needed.

And maybe he was right. It was time to get on with the day. With the future ahead of them. Starting with him finding Humphrey Kelly and her successfully prosecuting Wes Westmore.

In her spare time, she'd start looking at apartments.

They hadn't even made it to her office door before Cormac's phone rang.

"Maxwell made you after your visit to him," Sean said. "He admits following you to a restaurant, where you met Emily, and then following you home. He says she deserves to die, and he was planning to go after her next. But he swears he didn't send her any notes, flowers or a cradle."

"He's lying," Cormac said, stating the obvious. "Stalking is a sentence aggravator."

"We've already got him for two counts of premeditated murder…" Sean started in with the normal debate they seemed to go through anytime they worked together, and Cormac cut him off.

"He admits to seeing us at the restaurant," he said, just needing it done. "And we'd stopped to look at baby paraphernalia on the way in."

"He says he followed you to the restaurant, that Emily met you there."

That had happened, too. Since he'd had them under surveillance, it tracked that he'd seen them more than once.

"He's lying because he's one bitter, hateful, angry sucker," Cormac said then, and he realized he should have just let his brother talk. Thinking that Emily's life was in danger…

He was still a bit edgy. Wanted her out of there and back at his apartment, at least until they figured out their next step.

"I'm just giving you a heads-up as to what the prosecutor's office is going to hear on this one, because chances are Emily's going to be hearing about it sooner rather than later. I figured it would be better coming from you."

Oh. Right. Because he'd told his family that he and Emily were having a baby. They'd assumed that meant they were a couple, too.

He was getting the lowdown on behalf of his supposed partner. As a special privilege.

He didn't hate it.

"Killing Emily, finishing the job, is all the guy can talk about. I think him saying he didn't do the warnings is his way of keeping some hold over her. He aims to torment her with the possibility that she's still being hunted."

Sean's theory made a hell of a lot more sense than a guy up for double homicide worrying about aggravators.

"I'm assuming that his financials are currently under scrutiny?" he asked, wanting all ends tied up tightly, as he rode the elevator with Emily down to the ground floor. "I'd like to see confirmation of the cradle purchase." Since, so far, they'd still been unable to trace the cradle purchase through channels available to them.

Sean verified that someone was going through Maxwell's bank account and credit card statements, and then, as he and Emily waved to the uniformed officer at the private side exit of the DA's office, said, "By the way, James Kinney, he's back in custody. Parole violation. Been there since night before last."

The last name on the list.

They'd done it. But he hung up the phone before stepping outside. He would only breathe a sigh of relief when he had Emily safely home with him.

He saw the black car he'd hired for the day as soon as the door opened. With an arm around Emily's back, standing in close so she was protected, he reached down to pull open the back door.

But before he'd even grasped the handle, the door flew open from the inside, hitting him so hard it stunned him. Head, hand and right knee. In the same second, he felt a lurch, heard a shrill scream, and, through stars in his eyes, caught one glance at Emily's terrified face as she was pulled into the car that sped off even before the back door was fully closed.

Emily came to in a bizarre little room, like something out of one of those theme park rides that went in a tunnel and turned into some magical other world. Except that there was nothing magical about being supine on a bed she didn't recognize, with a headache so fierce she could hardly focus.

The baby!

Hand to her belly, she prayed that her baby still lay safely within her. With a frantic glance, she saw that she was still wearing the gray pantsuit she'd had on that morning. She'd had to pin the top button of the pants and it was still pinned exactly as she'd left it. Behind the button where it didn't show.

So it looked like the pants were buttoned.

And there was no wetness down below. No blood anywhere around her.

Thank God.

She hadn't lost the baby.

And didn't feel at all crampish.

As initial panic subsided, she moved her head enough to take in her space. Maybe ten by ten. Block walls, painted beige. A basement room? Basement apartment. There was no door she could see. Only what looked like an attic cover on the ceiling above. She was on a double bed, with a brocade comforter. There was an old-fashioned rocking chair in seemingly beautiful condition. A brocade sofa in what appeared to be a little sitting area, with an antique coffee table complete with a shiny silver tea set in the center of it.

As she rolled a bit, she made out a maroon, beige-and-brown-paisley-type carpet covering every inch of the floor.

There was a small counter with a sink on the far wall.

A table barely big enough for the two chairs pushed up to it. And, in the far corner, a room divider, bent in half, maybe a foot for each half, sectioning off a square foot.

The lighting was low—and came from a lamp on the living room table. Her coat hung on the wall opposite the end of the bed.

Sitting up, thinking she would get to her coat as a first step and then figure out the second, or at least, be ready when Cormac came for her, she saw the corner of the room previously blocked from her view by the footboard of the bed.

A cradle, exactly like the one pictured on the boxed gift that had been sent to her, was set up with a white satin-trimmed blanket lying neatly over the side.

That's when horror really struck.

And Emily started to pray.

Two seconds was all it took for Cormac to get his wits back about him. Two seconds too late. The license plate of the car, same make and model as the one he'd ordered that morning, was smudged with dirty snow. He couldn't make it out.

He had Sean on the line before the thing had turned the corner, and, within less than a minute, an APB went out to all units in the area to apprehend the car.

It should have been done by the time he hung up the phone.

Except that it wasn't.

Several black cars were stopped. Searched even. None of them had a kidnapped woman in the back seat or trunk.

The only woman in any of the cars had been a man's sick wife, a blonde, who'd been asleep with her head on his lap as he drove her to the hospital. The guy had been completely cooperative, showed his ID, allowed law enforcement to search his car, and they'd let him go.

It wasn't until half an hour later that someone realized that the ID the guy had been using belonged to a security guard who'd been stationed outside the courthouse.

A man who was missing.

He'd never shown up at the hospital. Nor was he at the address on file for him.

He also wasn't married.

The sick woman in the car…it had to have been Emily. With a hat, or a wig, that made her appear blonde.

Going with the theory that made the most sense, that Maxwell had someone working with him, someone who'd taken out the guard and used his credentials to grab Emily, they immediately went back to the officer who had spoken to the guy using the guard's ID. Got what information they could. "So we have a description of what the guy looks like," Cormac said, pacing in Sean's office as his brother relayed information as it came in.

Blond, blue eyes. Five-eleven. One hundred and sixty pounds.

It wasn't enough. He had to have something more solid. Couldn't just run willy-nilly through the snowy streets of New York accosting every blond guy he saw.

Think, man. Use your brain. You were close to the guy. He remembered seeing stars—and Emily's face.

Now was not the time to go blind.

What did he know?

What had they missed?

"This guy, had to have been working with Maxwell, not knowing that the man was in custody ," he said aloud, for the fourth time. He couldn't believe he hadn't seen it. There had to have been something...

That's why they weren't connecting Emily's abductor to the cradle. His partner had probably bought the roses, too. Hell, maybe it's the guard. Maybe the guy had been around during Maxwell's trial. Had his own issues with the lack of justice.

And a guard on the take could more easily explain how Maxwell had managed to keep them under surveillance so much of the time without being seen. More likely, though, they were dealing with an accomplice who'd taken down the guard. Posed as him.

"Someone he met in prison," he said, talking not to be heard—Sean already knew it all—but to get his thoughts in line.

Maxwell was being brought over from holding. The only reason Cormac was still in the building was because he was going to be allowed in on the interview.

"Here's the list," Sean said, taking a sheet off the printer.

Cormac's gaze sped over the names of Maxwell's known prison associates with a quick glance. He knew by heart the names on Emily's list of recently released convicts she'd been associated with.

If there was any mercy left on earth, the same name would hit both lists.

It did not.

So his accomplice was just someone he knew? A

friend? Someone he'd met in prison not associated with Emily? Why would anyone risk their life that way when no money was involved? What would be in it for them?

Every moment he spent standing there could be the one moment between life and death for Emily. And their baby.

He couldn't just wait around, doing nothing while she…

"He's here," Sean said, hanging up the landline phone on his desk as he led the way out of the office. Cormac knew his way. Waited only long enough for Sean to get them in the door of the small room with a table and two chairs on each side, and he was in front of the lined face, staring down dark brown eyes that seemed to be devoid of emotion.

"Where is she?" he asked without preamble. The man had already been read his rights when he'd been arrested. Cormac had no time for protocol.

Maxwell threw up both hands and shrugged.

And Cormac recognized his mistake. The more uptight he got, the more pleasure he gave the prisoner. The more victory.

Sitting down, he waited while Sean joined him, and then, pulling on the interview he'd already done with the guy, back when Maxwell had been in janitor garb, he asked, "You really going to let your partner get away with your spoils? Seriously? Again? You sit in jail while life goes on out here and others enjoy what belongs to you?"

"I don't know what in the hell you're talking about."

There. Petulance. He had Maxwell's attention.

"Your partner sure does."

Maxwell's sneer was unbecoming. "I have no partner. Isn't that the point?"

"So someone else just happens to abduct ADA Hernandez the morning that you're taken off the street." Cormac didn't ask. He stated. With obvious sarcasm.

That's when things screwed up. Maxwell's face lit up. He grinned. Glee came into his eyes.

And it made no sense.

"Seriously?" the man asked, his delight way too intense to be feigned. "So there is a God in heaven."

Leaning in, Sean said, "You weren't in on it?"

"No, but I sure as hell wish I was," the man said, still grinning. "Ha! He succeeded!"

"Who?"

"Hell if I know, but if you ever figure it out, let me know and I'll send the guy the rest of my life savings."

Cormac needed the ex-accountant to be lying. It was the only thing that made any sense.

But he didn't think he was. With a glance at Sean, he got the same message from his brother.

"When the guy went for her the first time, I was pissed," Maxwell was saying, obviously taking delight in their confusion, and in his ability to add to it simply by telling the truth. "I was making plans, good ones. The kind that left no room for mistakes. But then I heard on the news about the near abduction of an ADA, found out it was her, which made sense to me, and had to ramp up my plans. I wanted to be the one to do it to her, you know?"

Sobering, Maxwell looked between the two of them as though he actually expected them to understand.

Ready to puke, Cormac bailed from the room.

Chapter 23

An hour passed. Then two. Her bag wasn't in the room. She had to assume her phone had already been ditched. But she still had the watch on her wrist that her parents had given her for Christmas a couple of years before.

She could tell time. A way to stay connected to the outside world.

The headache was mostly gone. She'd explored her space. Had seen the portable toilet behind the small screen. In the bottom of the cupboard, she'd found an apartment-sized refrigerator stocked with milk, juice, and fresh fruits and vegetables. The upper cupboard held crackers, peanut butter, other snacks, and cups and plates. Two of each.

It didn't take her long to realize plans had been made to keep her, or someone, in that hole for a length of time.

Nine months?

That cradle in the corner upset her most of all.

She avoided looking in that direction.

She had figured out that someone who knew she was pregnant was planning to see that her baby was born healthy.

And the only reason she could come up with for that was that whoever it was would then take the baby from her.

Walking around the room, she looked closely at the walls, searching for any sign that might have been left by a previous occupant. Another pregnant woman?

An older woman, like her, who the kidnapper had decided wasn't fit to be a mother?

Or another single woman?

Her mind was running away with her, she knew it. But why would someone who wanted revenge, wanted her dead, dump her in a homey looking room?

He knew about the baby. The whole cradle thing…

He wanted her baby!

No. Dropping to the bed, she started to shake again. Clasped her hands together and remembered Cormac reaching for her hand earlier that day. Remembered his strength. He was counting on her to keep his baby safe and she was not going to let him down.

The man had already suffered enough for one lifetime.

If anything happened to her or the baby, he'd blame himself. Just as he had with Willa. She'd looked up the case. The woman's death had been fully on her. She'd been a consummate actress. Not just with Cormac, but with the high-ranking law enforcement officers with whom she worked, as well as with cartel leaders.

But that hadn't stopped him from thinking he'd missed something.

Because he was that hard on himself. Expected that much out of himself.

Someone besides Cormac had known about the baby, even before he'd told his siblings that morning.

Maxwell had known.

The cradle. The notes.

He had to have an accomplice…

A noise from above made her jerk. Hard enough to pull something in her neck. She was so stiff with tension she was surprised she didn't just break. When the sound came again, from the panel in the ceiling, she jumped up from the bed.

If someone thought they were going to…

No. She would not let her emotions get control of her. She was better than that. Fear would put her baby at risk.

It made no sense that anyone would be expecting to share the bed with her, she told herself, an effort to stay calm. If what they were after was a healthy baby, they had to leave her alone.

That's the card she'd play if they tried to touch her.

And if she had to, she'd find something to murder the guy. The milk and juice cartons were cardboard. Paper plates and cups and plastic silverware, she'd figured for ease of cleaning—just toss them—but maybe so she wouldn't have a weapon.

The lamp was part of the table. She'd need a saw to get it loose.

But there was the light bulb. She'd have to be sure of her escape route once she unscrewed it. There were no windows. She'd be plunged into complete darkness.

What about a bar from the refrigerator rack? If she could find a way to break it free…

A louder crack sounded, and, heart thudding, Emily moved as far away from the panel as she could. She stood on the other side of the eating table, figuring she could pull it on its side, use it as a shield.

Thinking. She had to keep thinking.

The panel came away, and, worried she might be sick, Emily watched the square hole in the ceiling, trying to be prepared for whatever might come down.

A tray appeared with a rope tied around it, and a voice sounded just to the right of her head. "I made pasta and salad for you," the male voice said, as though he was her waiter serving her in a restaurant. As though all he wanted to do was please her.

"Who are you?"

"You know who I am," he said.

But she didn't. She really, really didn't.

"I'll be joining you, in time," the voice continued, and she started searching the cupboard. "It's underneath," he said then.

And she stared at the tray he'd lowered to the floor.

"The speaker. That's what you're looking for, right?"

She couldn't see him, and there was no way he could see her through the opening in the ceiling, either.

"You have a camera on me?"

He'd been watching her the entire time she'd been there? She should have figured that one.

"I have to know if you're in trouble or need something," he said. "But don't worry, I have it positioned so that you can use the restroom in private."

Good to know. For what reason, she wasn't yet sure, but knew she'd figure it out.

"What do you want from me?"

"It's okay, Emily, you don't need to play shy with me. You know what I want. What we both want. You just need a bit to get used to the idea. I understand that. Time locked up alone will give you that. You'll see. You'll come around. And when you do, I'll be here waiting. We'll be married, and raise our child, and live a good and happy life."

The guy was deranged.

The notes.

Her stalker.

Maxwell's accomplice was a nutjob.

But if she played along, would he leave her alone? He'd said she had to be locked alone…so, for the moment, to stay alive, and untouched, she just had to play the game?

Give Cormac time to find her so he didn't blame himself…

But the baby…

She needed an ultrasound…to know that everything was okay…to know if something else needed to be done…

It wasn't scheduled for another week. So not the moment's problem.

The baby. She'd been drugged. She didn't want to interact with the man. Wasn't going to give him the pleasure. But she needed to know. "What did you give me?"

She should have made herself throw up the second she'd awoken.

"Just my own concoction, mostly natural. Don't worry, I just covered your nose and mouth with it long enough to knock you out. I wouldn't do anything to harm our baby, Emily. You can trust me on that."

She wanted to. Oh, God, how she wanted to.

"Thank you."

"See? You're already starting to come around."

She wasn't. Would never. No matter how long he held her captive.

"I'm really sorry about all of this," the voice came again. "I didn't want it to happen this way."

Then why was the room there? It definitely hadn't come to be overnight. She couldn't let herself start to believe him. To think she needed him.

Stockholm syndrome could set in. She'd start to sympathize with him and—

No.

"It's just, when I saw you leave his apartment with him today, I knew I could no longer trust you…"

What had made him think he could trust her in the first place?

Had she seen him, not knowing he was Maxwell's accomplice? Had he approached Maxwell, offering to help?

Did they know each other in prison?

All questions she wouldn't ask. But she wouldn't stop thinking them. She'd keep her mind working. Use her mental assets. Keep herself sharp.

"Now, untie your dinner so I can pull the rope back up. Unless you want me to come down there and do it for you?"

She didn't want that. With lightning speed she retrieved the tray, got back over by the wall and watched as the rope disappeared into the hole in the ceiling.

"Enjoy the pasta," the voice said, then the panel slid back in place.

Feeling a small sense of relief—at least the man wasn't going to be joining her—she promised herself that she wouldn't become emotionally or mentally dependent upon him.

Physically, she had to eat. She might lose her dinner, but she had to eat. The baby needed nourishment. And so Emily helped herself to a plastic fork and sat down at the table, forcing herself to chew and swallow.

Her job was clear for the moment: keep herself and the baby as healthy as possible.

Keep them alive. Maintain complete control of her mind.

And pray that Cormac found her before more than a tray came down through that hole.

It was a nightmare that didn't end. He was back to the beginning, only instead of preventing the kidnapping of the ADA he'd gone to visit, he'd been right there with her, supposedly protecting her, when she was snatched.

Right out of his arms…

Police had been in touch with the owner of the car service he'd used to hire the day's car. Had spoken with the driver, who said that a man had come out of the DA's office, told him that Cormac was involved in police business and wouldn't be needing the car anymore that day, and paid him a hundred bucks in cash for his trouble.

The only description he had of the guy was medium height and build, black or brown winter coat, hood and scarf.

Law enforcement was working on securing traffic cam and private surveillance footage around the area, trying to track the car that had driven away with Emily inside.

Who'd have believed it would be so easy to get one over on Cormac Colton?

Shaking with fury, Cormac shut himself up in a room at the precinct and began poring over every piece of evidence pertaining to Emily, from Sean's printed and digital files.

He laid Emily's list of anyone she thought might have a beef against her in the center of the table, glancing up at it as he scourged through information.

He wanted the notes that had come with the gifts, the email the perp had sent, all in front of him. Printed them off.

Stared at them for about two minutes before something struck him.

A memory. Niggling.

But nothing to do with the case.

The verbiage, the ownership and the conciliatory tone…

Cold to the core…he knew. Had to get home, to his computer. To reread an email not in the case file. Telling Sean that he'd be in touch, he ran from the building, and, slipping and sliding on the snow-slick sidewalks, he ran until he saw a free cab, too. He was barreling through his apartment door in record time.

Their computers were right where they'd left them.

He swallowed hard, refused to take in the cozy scene and went straight for his computer. Punching the keys with much more force than they deserved.

The email appeared. He read. And saw red.

Six o'clock. She'd had dinner. Had thrown away the packaging and utensil. And panicked when she realized how quickly that little trash bin was going to fill up. Someone would have to come down to take out the trash. She broke down the plastic container that had come down on the tray. Next time she'd empty whatever came down, sending most of the trash back up.

If there was a next time.

But it was a plan. A good plan. She'd collect her trash and send it back up with the dining tray. Yes, that would work.

You'll see, little one. You and I, we'll be resource-

ful. We'll figure it out one step at a time. That's how life is. When things seem overwhelming, or you feel like you might be losing a case, you take things one step at a time. And if the loss becomes clear, you look for the deal. The compromise.

Everyone needs something. We just have to figure out what our captor needs. And hope it's different than what he thinks he wants, because that we will not be giving to him.

She spoke to her baby silently, unwilling to take a chance that her captor was listening to every sound she made.

And to that end, she refused to cry out loud. When tears threatened, she buried her head in the cupboard.

Or stepped behind the screen.

He might have lied about the portable toilet area not being on camera. She didn't think so. Her captor seemed more deranged than filled with bone-deep evil. Hate.

Or, he could be playing her, stringing her along.

Behind the screen, she wiped away tears. Longing for Cormac. Longing to be trapped in his apartment forever and ever.

He was a strong man. Independent as they came. He wouldn't let her break his heart.

And when it came to understanding the dregs of humanity, the lows to which people would sink, Cormac already knew it all. Maybe even better than she did. Living with her, listening to her, wasn't going to make him an ounce more jaded than he already was.

And the age thing…funny how, when one faced the possibility of imminent death, age mattered not at all.

She'd rather grow old sooner than he did, than not grow old at all. Cormac had a lot of doing left in front of him, and damn it, she wanted to be there to know about it. To cheer him on.

Placing her hand to her heart, as though she could squeeze back tears, Emily felt the front-closure clasp of her bra. Remembered how skilled Cormac was at flipping it open with a quick move of his fingers.

And…the bra.

Straps. A metal closure. Bras distracted men.

Within minutes she had the thing off, was working with it, trying different things. She couldn't stay in there too long. Wouldn't risk making whomever he was suspicious enough to come down. But she could go out and think a bit. Come back and forth.

Because one way or another, she was going to figure out how to make that piece of lingerie into a noose.

A weapon.

She would not stay in captivity in a dungeon unprotected.

Chapter 24

The application for one Peter Bezos to reapply for his license to practice law was being processed. Just like the man had said.

He wasn't out on parole. He was just out, so had no one to report to. And there was no known address for the man that anyone could readily find.

Sean was getting a warrant to open up the bar application, to find the address listed there.

The man had had no money left after paying the restitution to the people he'd helped his clients swindle, but he had paid in full, and there was no debt popping up in his name. No credit cards, either.

One could only assume he'd had assets stashed someplace like the Cayman Islands or had had cash hidden away and waiting for him someplace.

No wonder he'd been able to keep such a close eye on Emily. He'd been a shadow in the world. He'd drawn no attention to himself, outside of his attempts to connect with the ADA who put him away.

Bezos was smarter than the average guy.

But Cormac was smart, too. And he had a hell of a lot more at stake than the smarmy lawyer did.

He followed all the proper channels.

And then, an hour after he'd figured out who'd taken the mother of his baby—taken the woman who he suddenly didn't see himself living without—Cormac called his twin.

His ex-con brother had connections he didn't have. Old ones, to be sure, but old was better than none.

"What can I do?" Liam picked up the phone with the question. Sean had already filled their siblings in. And with a New York ADA missing, everyone in law enforcement would know soon, if they didn't already.

"I need to talk to someone who knew Bezos in prison," Cormac said. "A cellmate would be best, but anyone... someone he worked with in the kitchen. A guard..."

Liam's two-year stint had been served in the same prison that had housed Peter Bezos.

"I'll make some calls..."

The phone went dead.

But not for long. Cormac had his jacket back on and was heading out the door, on his way to talk to neighbors at the last known address for Bezos, when Liam called back.

"I'm out front," his twin said. "We need to take a drive."

Darkness met him at the door of his building, and Cormac's insides shook as he pictured his Emily alone with a crazed man. Spending the night with him.

He'd kill the guy. The second he saw him he was going to...

Do it right.

He would save Emily, save his kid and follow the rules so that, while Bezos wasted away behind bars, Cormac would be teaching his kid how to fly a kite.

And making love to Emily.

That's the ball he had to keep his eye on.

Anything else, imaginings, worries, they'd just distract him from his goal.

And that was not going to happen again.

She was not going to lie down on the bed. Ever. She wasn't even going to sit on it again. To do so would give her captor the sense that she was settling in.

And then he'd join her.

He was just waiting...

"You look tired, dear. Have a rest. The bed is new. A pillowtop. And has a gel foam mattress cover, too."

Jerking upright on the couch, lifting her head from the pillow she'd laid against the wall at the back of the couch, Emily felt her heart pounding like it was going to come up out of her chest.

He was watching her.

Wrapping her arms around herself, she snuggled into the sweater she'd put on that morning—was it still the same day she'd awoken in Cormac's spare bedroom? Had she been knocked out overnight?

Was Cormac ever going to find her?

If she made her captor mad, would he hurt her? Cause her to lose the baby?

She had to do whatever it took to keep her baby safe.

"You're making me feel violated, the way you're watching me," she said, finding a strength of voice she hadn't known she still possessed.

"I'm only checking in, I swear. Just to make certain you're okay. The last thing I want is to make you a victim of psychological manipulation." The legal term sat well with her.

"Oh, and you think kidnapping me and keeping me a prisoner in cement walls is better?" Yes. She had to stay pissed. The way she had when Blake Nygren had tried to intimidate her in court with his unending evil stares.

She'd won that case.

"Think of this as detox," the voice said, almost soothingly. "Trust me, you'll thank me later."

"When you're in prison?"

The man actually chuckled. Like a parent taking genuine humor from the innocent antics of a child.

And her tension eased a bit. He didn't seem like he meant her any harm. She'd checked for bruises on her body the first time she'd gone behind the screen, for any sign that she'd been touched in any way, and found none. He'd had her passed out, in a cell, and he'd left her alone.

"Mind if I ask your opinion on something?" The question came softly. Almost hesitantly. As though he was suddenly the underling, showing her respect.

Was it all a game? "Do I have a choice?"

"Of course."

She wanted to tell him to go away. To quit looking at her. Better yet, to let her go.

But maybe it would serve her better to hear his question. To pave a way into his mind enough that she could cut a deal for her way out of the nightmare he held her in.

"Go ahead and ask, I'm just sitting here."

And there followed the most bizarre thirty minutes. He brought up court cases, not just hers. And not just one type. They talked about civil procedures, evidentiary law as it applied to a well-known murder trial, and judge's rulings.

She was passing the time. Keeping panic at bay. Using her mind. Focusing.

"You see, my dear Emily. We've got a connection, even if you don't see it yet. I do. And I've got the plan…"

My dear Emily.

No.

Oh, God.

Bezos.

Lawyer with high-powered slimy clients. Some of whom managed to get away with murderous crimes, while he took the fall for them.

Who owed him.

He'd been playing her all along. Biding his time.

And after he got all he could out of traumatizing her mentally and emotionally, he was going to kill her. What other choice would he have? Either keep her down there until she died. Or she'd call the police.

He wanted her to suffer.

With a cradle in the corner as a reminder of all that she'd be losing.

Oh, God, Cormac…he'd suspected the guy and she'd insisted that Bezos wasn't their stalker.

She'd set Cormac up to fail.

And that broke her heart.

No one in the prison system wanted to talk about Peter Bezos. The man had connections. High up, powerful ones. Guards said they didn't know anything that could help. Just talked about how clean Peter Bezos kept his cell, how he spent a lot of his time in the prison library reading law books and how completely he followed all rules.

He was a model inmate.

Cormac believed them.

Inmates said a lot of the same but clammed up when he asked what Bezos had said when he talked about getting out. They knew nothing.

Funny thing was, no one had picked on the guy. He'd made it through his years in prison without a blemish.

He'd been protected, Cormac translated.

Liam agreed with him.

They'd wasted invaluable hours and gained nothing. Ten o'clock at night. Emily had to be frantic.

Or worse.

And the baby…

She was already at risk and…

Her blood pressure…

He hadn't told her he loved her.

Cormac was busy swallowing that revelation, when Liam said, "I know who we need to speak to," and, gathering his things from the prison room where they'd been conducting interviews, finished with, "Come on."

He didn't have a chance to ask where they were going as Liam collected his personal items from the bin and immediately dialed his phone.

Cormac didn't much care where they went as long as Liam was leading them to answers.

To any hope at all that he'd get Emily and the baby back alive.

"One of the prison librarians, he's an ex-con who volunteers," Liam said as he jumped behind the wheel of the vehicle he'd driven to pick up Cormac.

"He's willing to speak with us?"

"Yep. I did his kid a solid a few years back," Liam said, and sped off into the night.

She couldn't sleep. Would not turn off the light.

She'd spent half an hour conversing with her captor as though they were work associates.

Bezos was that good.

A savvy lawyer with the gift of con. He'd played her in court. Looking back, she saw that.

And he was still playing her. All the nice things in her hellhole, the concession he'd made to privacy for her voiding needs…even a sink. But there was no soap of any kind. No washcloths, towels, toothbrush, toothpaste. No change of clothes.

She'd have to ask him for the things she'd need. And then feel just a little bit grateful once she'd received them.

He wanted control of her mind, and for a few minutes that evening he'd had it.

He was going for Stockholm syndrome. She'd already figured that much out. But what if, even knowing, she couldn't prevent it from happening?

He knew she'd do anything to save her baby.

Eat his food. Engage in his conversation.

What more was he going to ask of her?

How much was she willing to compromise herself to stay alive?

And the alternative?

To die on Cormac's watch?

She'd be committing the man to his own private hell for the rest of his life.

Leaning forward on the couch, she cradled her mostly flat belly with her arms. Laid her head down on them.

Saw her boots.

And knew what she had to do.

If the worst happened, Cormac needed to know that it was her fault. Not his.

She'd been so certain Peter Bezos was a decent enough guy, deserving of a second chance.

Crossing to the screen in the corner of the room, she sat, fully clothed, on the toilet seat, unzipped her boot, and with the corner of the small metal grasp, she began carving into the cement wall of her prison.

And when she started to worry about her captor getting suspicious with her being gone for so long, assuming he was still awake, she left the screened area long enough to fluff the pillows on the bed, turn down the covers, and turn out the light.

Her eyes would adjust to the darkness.

And if they didn't, she had her fingers to guide her.

She had a name to carve and might only have the one night to do it.

Bezos.

If she had time, she had something else she had to tell Cormac, too.

If she had time.

"The guy was deranged, if you ask me." Lincoln Miller sat at the plastic-topped table in his kitchen, sipping from the coffee he'd had ready for all three of them when Liam and Cormac arrived. The man's calloused fingers, his ruddy skin, didn't speak nearly as loudly as the kindness in his blue eyes.

Cormac needed more than kindness. Sean had called to let him know that Bezos had put down an apartment number in Emily's building as his address on the license application. The apartment was vacant. Up for rent.

"I did some bad things in my youth," Lincoln was saying, "but I knew they were wrong. This Bezos guy, he thinks if he says something, it's so. Like he can convince anyone of anything and then life goes his way. And when it comes to Ms. Hernandez, he was the one who was convinced. He'd talk about how she'd gone easy on him in court, and how he knew it was because she was sweet on him. Said they had a connection."

Cormac needed the coffee but didn't sip. He wasn't sure he could swallow.

"When she wrote a letter to the parole board on his behalf, it, like, tipped him over the edge. He said she was his way back in to practicing law. Enough time had passed for him to reapply for his license, and he really thought the bar association would reinstate him. With an ADA's backing, why wouldn't they?"

Lincoln's tired gaze moved from one to the other of them, his shoulders encased in an off-white long undershirt.

On the way over, Liam had told Cormac the man lived alone. Collected minimal social security. And yet, he seemed more at peace, more satisfied with his place in life than almost anyone Liam had ever known.

"He said he'd get her to marry him, and that status was going to build back his clientele."

Growing sicker, more enraged, by the moment, Cormac was finding it difficult not to push his seat back hard against the linoleum and get the hell out of there.

To where?

"Did he give you any indication about his finances? Did he have money stashed?" They had to have a starting place to find the guy.

"Not specifically, but money didn't seem to be on his

mind much. It was getting his high-powered status back that consumed him."

"You wouldn't happen to know of any relatives he has? Anyplace he might go…"

Lincoln was shaking his head, and then, stopped. Eyes wide, he stared at the two of them.

"There was this book…" he started. Then stopped.

Cormac about came out of his skin.

"What book?" he asked, channeling his adrenaline to school his tone.

"I noticed because it wasn't a lawbook, which was all he ever looked at," Lincoln said, sitting up straighter. "It was a construction manual. And he said he'd inherited a place outside the city. It was a dump, he wouldn't want anyone knowing about it, but he was thinking maybe he'd fix it up as some kind of fancy summer home…"

"Where?" Cormac's chair shot behind him as he stood. He quickly righted it and slid it up to the table, his knuckles white against the top of it.

Lincoln shook his head. "That's what I'm trying to remember…anything he might have said that would give you guys a clue…"

"He said summer home," Liam piped in, standing as well. "Was it on the water?"

Eyes widening again, Lincoln looked up at the brothers. "He was reading about saltwater damage. I remember because I used to have a boat."

Cormac listened as his brother thanked the older man. Profusely. He was still trying to find words to express his own gratitude when Lincoln stood. "And something else," the man said, frowning. "The place was from his mother's side of the family."

The buzzer in Cormac's brain rang. Pulling out his

phone, he called his older brother for access to Peter Bezos's birth certificate.

And within the hour had Bezos's mother's maiden name.

It was Smith.

Over five hundred homes situated near the ocean within an hour of the city came up under that name.

It could take him weeks to find the right one.

Chapter 25

Leaning her head back against the cement wall, Emily closed her eyes. Just for a second. Her carving was almost done. She needed a *C*. That was all.

She'd tried to take a nap sometime during the night. With no light on, she'd lost track of time. For that matter, she might have had days and nights mixed up from the moment she first awoke in her cell. It might not have been the middle of the night for all she knew.

Maybe she ate pasta before six in the morning, instead of late afternoon.

Maybe she was going to die.

Her head ached. From gritting her teeth while she carved. From tension. From crying.

And maybe from whatever Bezos had doused her with when he'd abducted her.

She had to get her *C* done and get out of the bathroom.

She couldn't let him find her there. Or let him see her notes. He'd paint over them. Or scrape them away.

She felt again, mid wall, up where it would be easily seen.

Bezos. Her fingers made out the rudimentary letters, and then dropped to her lap. The skin frayed.

She reached out again, by her shoulder, at the edge of the screen, where she'd been sitting for hours and hours. Felt her last words, if it came to that.

She raised her stinging fingers, ignoring the cramps as she held the broken zipper up to the wall. Making an upright half circle. Over and over and over. Uncaring that her knuckles grazed the wall with each stroke.

She just wanted to finish.

And to close her eyes…

Thunder sounded. Jerking, her back ramrod straight against the wall, Emily stared into the darkness. Had that sound been in her head, or…

No…it was still there.

Definitely thunder. Far away. Then seemingly right above her. Then farther away again.

Thunder in February?

Or…had she been down there for months? Had he kept her knocked out so she thought it was only a day?

Had she needed to believe it was a day so she let reality slip?

God, she was tired.

And…her belly was still mostly flat.

But not completely flat. Her button still had the pin in it.

She took a deep breath. Shuddered. Felt the tears dripping out from the corners of her eyes. She wasn't some coed with a body young enough to spend the night on cold cement without aching in every part of her. She was closer to fifty than thirty.

And…

She was pregnant with Cormac's baby. They were counting on her to make their family. She had to…

The sound came again. Sharper. Followed by an angry male voice.

Bezos must have figured out she wasn't in the bed. And hadn't been for some time. Maybe his camera had an infrared lens.

Pulse beating in her throat, she tried to stand. Almost fell from the stiffness in her limbs. Crawled out to the main room, while the man continued to yell.

She opened her mouth to yell back. To tell him that she was right there. Wondered why he didn't just use the speaker.

A bang sounded, just as the ceiling panel cracked, letting light into the room. Huddled in the far corner of the couch, Emily held her noose behind the pillow she was clutching with her free hand and waited.

She'd practiced with the pillow.

She might only get once chance and she was going to get it right.

A loud crack sounded, different, just as something hit the side of her arm, hard. And there he was, Bezos, sliding down the rope.

He'd finished waiting.

She was so tired. Her arm was stinging, her hands ached, but for Cormac, for their baby, she had to find the strength.

She'd only have the one chance.

The shape came toward her in the dark, but she couldn't let herself look at him. Couldn't afford to hesitate. As soon as he was within reaching distance, bending over to grab her up, she pounced upward, yanked with all her might, and, as her bra circled his neck, she tugged for all she was worth.

Overdosing on adrenaline laced with fear, Cormac held the material away from his larynx with one hand and reached out toward Emily with the other.

He was afraid that whatever Bezos had done to her couldn't be undone. And he needed to grab her up, to promise her she'd never have to fear the man again.

"Emily...it's okay, Em," he said. Stumbling over a lack of words. Throat clogged, not from her noose, but with emotion, he moved in closer to her. "It's me, Em. You're okay now. You're safe," he said, as he felt the pressure against the fingers at his neck subside.

"Light, I need light!" he screamed when she didn't speak.

"Em?" He felt for her face. There were tears there, but no other movement. "Em? Stay with me," he cried out, hearing his own panic.

Hearing a shuffle behind him, he continued to take stock of Emily with his hands, afraid of what he'd find, but knowing he might have little time to help her.

"The medic's on his way down." Liam's voice sounded right behind him as the room flooded with light.

And that's when he saw the blood staining the side of Emily's left upper arm. Fresh blood. Oozing. Most likely made worse by the pressure she'd used to try to strangle him.

"She's been shot!" Ripping at her sleeve, while Liam supported her arm, he tore his way down to the wound.

"Looks like only a graze," Liam said. "The devil, Bezos. Had to go down shooting."

The man lay in another pool of blood just above them. His own blood. From the gunshot wound one of the officers who'd come in with them had given him when he'd pulled his own gun to shoot through the floor by the panel they'd just found.

Sliding an arm gently around Emily's back, Cormac lifted her forward and felt her stir.

"It's okay, Em," he said again. "You're safe now."

"Cormac?" He didn't recognize the voice. It was little more than croak, but more, she sounded beaten. Scared to death and… "Did I get him?" she asked, and then, her eyes open and focusing, stared at the apparatus around his neck.

He hadn't bothered to remove it. He'd had more pressing details on his mind. Like the blood-smeared hands she raised up to his neck.

"I…" Frowning, he saw the total confusion on her face.

And Liam grabbed the makeshift rope around his neck. "Yep, this is the woman for you, bro," he said, breaking the tension that was about to shatter Cormac. "It's her bra! Good thinking, Emily Hernandez, and welcome to the family."

Emily blinked, squinted, and glanced between Liam and Cormac. She didn't grin, but he felt her relax against his arm as he held her. "I thought you were Bezos," she said weakly, closing her eyes briefly, and then opening them again. "It was him, Cormac. You were right to be suspicious and I got played." The words came out in a rush.

He opened his mouth to tell her she was anything but played. She, with her bra noose and her Herculean inner strength, was the only woman he wanted beside him throughout life. But the medics climbed down the ladder Liam must have lowered into the small walled-off basement alcove—a construction job that had led them to the right Smith house—and were pushing him away as they took Emily's vitals.

"Hey, bro, come look at this," Liam said, from across the small space. He was looking behind a small room divider screen.

Needing to tell the paramedics that Emily was pregnant, but not sure she still was, he went to see what his twin had found.

He saw the blood smeared all over the wall first, and his gut, his heart, sank. She'd lost the baby…

Then Liam pointed to the indentations in the wall. A roughly carved *Bezos*. Naming her captor, making certain there was concrete evidence of her abductor. Proof that would stand up in court.

If it were possible to fall for the woman more, he'd have done so.

And then he followed Liam's finger down and over a bit. *I love Cormac.*

The woman had scraped her knuckles raw, must have spent most of the night doing it, to admit that she loved him…

Just at that moment, he heard Emily's voice in conversation with the paramedics. "I'm pregnant," she said, her lips barely moving, her eyes closed.

And Cormac, with tears in his eyes, and weak at the knees, bent his head with thanks.

Because of the baby, they wanted to keep Emily in the hospital overnight. She'd lost a lot of blood, been under far too much stress.

But the bullet injury was only a graze, just like Liam had said. It hurt like hell, but she'd take that any day as long as she and the baby were okay.

Her bandaged hands hurt worse. Maybe the whole carving idea had been a bit out there. Clearly, if anyone had ever found her down there, or found the cell at all, they'd have known who was in possession of the place.

And the rest…

When facing death, telling her truth had been what she'd had to do.

"Okay, you ready?" The nurse, Lily, was back in the emergency room cubicle she'd been lying in for what seemed like hours while different medical people were in and out fawning over her. "They're ready for you in Ultrasound…"

She was about to find out if her pregnancy was viable. And she had no idea where Cormac was.

Hadn't seen him since they'd loaded her in the ambulance.

Nodding, she pulled the sheet and flannel blanket covering her up to her chin, felt the bed start to move and saw a familiar figure push through a door at the end of the hall, with a nurse right behind him. "Sir, you can't go…"

"Cormac!" She called out to him, only afterward aware of others around her in the bustling department. But she was thrilled to see him.

Her bed stopped moving, Lily standing beside it, as a very bedraggled, wrinkled, smudged and tired-looking man came up to the bed. "I washed my hands," he said, to no one in particular.

"You're here," she said, staring up at him. And she started to cry. She reached up a gauze-covered hand, right there in the middle of the hall, touching his face, running the tips of her fingers along the neck she barely remembered trying to strangle, and just couldn't stop the flow.

"I'm here," he said. "I had to give a statement. Bezos is gone, Em. It's over. I got here as quickly as I could."

"Sir, I'm sorry, I know this is important, but we're on our way for a test that can't be put off. If you'll just wait in that cubicle, we'll have her right back—"

"No." Blinking away tears, Emily looked at Lily, and then back at Cormac. "He's the baby's father. He has a right to be there."

She watched as his eyes grew wide, and when he touched her shoulder, holding on to walk down the hall beside her bed, she covered his hand with her bandaged one.

She'd never had an ultrasound before. Might have been embarrassed as her gown was pulled up, and sheets arranged, so that her entire lower belly was exposed.

Except that Cormac had seen it all before.

And…a little bit of nudity just didn't matter when you'd come through the night she had.

The technician told her she'd feel a cold sensation as she applied gel. Then pointing to a monitor to Emily's left, she instructed them to watch if they wanted to, and started the procedure.

Cormac never left her side. "Whatever it is, Em, it's okay," he said, about thirty seconds in when nothing but snow seemed to be appearing on the screen.

"And I love you, too, by the way."

Shocked beyond words, her head jerked toward him and she stared open-mouthed up at him. The way those intense brown eyes bore into hers, she knew.

"You saw the wall."

"I have a picture of it on my phone that will be with me every day for the rest of my life," he told her.

"Here we go," the technician said, but before Emily even turned her head back to the screen, a sound came into the room. *Da. Duh. Da. Duh. Da. Duh.* Fast. But strong.

"We have a heartbeat?" she screeched, half sitting up to stare at the snowy screen.

"And a sac, a fetus and a yolk," the technician said, pointing out each, while tears ran down Emily's cheeks. Her baby was viable.

Cormac's fingers wiped at her tears. But she felt one drop, too, onto her hand, and knew that she wasn't the only one filled with supreme, overflowing gratitude.

The technician took measurements. Made notes. Wiped off Emily's stomach, covered her back with the sheet, and, with a big smile, said that someone would be in shortly to take her back to the ER.

"We have a baby," she said, mostly breathless, tearful, afraid to believe.

"Now can we tell your parents??" He pointed to the screen. "I was told out in the ER that we can get photos of that."

"You do realize that my parents will be flying up the second they hear."

"I'm looking forward to meeting them. And assuring them that you and the baby will be well loved and protected."

Growing serious, Emily teared up. "I have no doubt about that, you know. You'll be right here with us every step of the way. I know it in my heart. I love you, Cormac."

Cormac stood there in his day-old clothes, with a

growth of stubble and tears on his face, his fingers caressing her cheek as he spoke. "I love you, too. Forever. And now, ADA Emily Hernandez, will you please say you'll marry me?"

"Yes, Mr. Colton. I will."

* * * * *

Don't miss the first book in the Coltons of New York miniseries:

Colton's Unusual Suspect
by Marie Ferrarella

Available now from Harlequin Romantic Suspense

And don't miss

Colton's Body Of Proof
by Karen Whiddon,

Coming next month!

HARLEQUIN
PLUS

Try the best multimedia subscription service for romance readers like you!

Read, Watch and Play.

Experience the easiest way to get the romance content you crave.

Start your **FREE TRIAL** at
<u>www.harlequinplus.com/freetrial</u>.